OF GRIF

'My name is Steven
can see it written in the
out the New York subway system and especially on the side of the escalator in the Brooklyn High Street station near my house. I am, in fact, "the mild-mannered, bespectacled art student" who "masterminded the Great Graffiti Caper", as the newspapers called our little adventure last spring. A flattering description, but neither true nor fair to the three other masterminds who deserve an equal share of the glory and the blame. What follows is meant to set the record straight and to satisfy any lingering curiosity about this absurd but gratifying affair.'

This fast-paced, topical and very funny story of how Steve Wiley and his friends stage the most daring graffiti caper of the century is Kate Gilmore's first novel. It is a gripping read, and guaranteed to have you on the edge of your seat!

Kate Gilmore lives in Brooklyn, New York. She is married to a mathematician and computer enthusiast and has lived in many different parts of the world. She has two children; one is an artist whose activities were largely the inspiration for this book! When she is not writing or shopping for exotic ingredients for her husband to cook, Kate Gilmore enjoys playing the French horn.

KATE GILMORE

OF GRIFFINS AND GRAFFITI

PUFFIN BOOKS

For Geoffrey

Puffin Books, Penguin Books Ltd, Harmondsworth, Middlesex, England
Viking Penguin Inc., 40 West 23rd Street, New York, New York 10010, U.S.A.
Penguin Books Australia Ltd, Ringwood, Victoria, Australia
Penguin Books Canada Limited, 2801 John Street, Markham, Ontario, Canada L3R 1B4
Penguin Books (N.Z.) Ltd, 182–190 Wairau Road, Auckland 10, New Zealand

First published 1987

Made and printed in Great Britain by
Richard Clay Ltd,
Bungay, Suffolk
Typeset in Ehrhardt

My name is Steven Wiley. My name is SABRE 75. You can see it written in the now familiar, stylish script throughout the New York subway system and especially off the side of the escalator in the Brooklyn High Street station near my house. I am, in fact, 'the mild-mannered, bespectacled art student' who 'masterminded the Great Graffiti Caper', as the newspapers called our little adventure last spring. A flattering description, but neither true nor fair to the three other masterminds who deserve an equal share of glory and of blame. What follows is meant to set the record straight and to satisfy any lingering curiosity about this absurd but gratifying affair.

CHAPTER 1

It all began on a Saturday night which was much like any other Saturday night. There was nothing to mark it as a night which would live in infamy – no pricking of my thumbs, no prodigies appearing in the murky skies over Manhattan. I had, as usual, spent my allowance, which was dispensed on Monday, and I faced with very little fortitude a weekend at home. Being at home is not without its solitary pleasures such as reading and drawing and watching the tube, but there is something about having to stay home for lack of funds that drives me swiftly round the bend. At ten o'clock, just when I had become almost desperate enough to contemplate a walk through the deadly gentility of Brooklyn Heights, Dorc called and saved my sanity.

Dorc is my closest friend. He is also older, taller, better looking and the constant companion of a rather beautiful girl. For these reasons I had not thought of him as a source of amusement on a dull Saturday night.

My mother handed me the phone which I had not even bothered to answer.

'Speak!' I growled into it, in the somewhat painful bass I used on such occasions.

'What's up, man?' Dorc said.

'Nothing much,' I replied. 'What's up with you?'

'Nothing,' Dorc said. 'Nothing's up. Nothing's ever up. You've got to come hang out, man. Immediately. Before I die of boredom. I am drawing my last breath.' There were sounds of labored breathing on the line.

'Where's Sonia?' I asked unsympathetically. 'That's her job.'

'Not home, faithless female. Will may come, but then again he may not, and you're closer.'

'Flattery will get you nowhere,' I said, 'but let me see if I can get the subway fare. I've done it again with the money.'

I turned with a wheedling expression all prepared and found my mother standing there with a handful of change and a resigned smile on her face. As I said, this was a Saturday night just like a lot of others. She had probably gone for the rescue funds when she heard Dorc's voice on the phone.

'All right, it's cool,' I said. 'Don't do anything desperate. I'm on my way.'

'Call when you start home,' my mother said as I was pulling on my coat.

'Don't I always?'

'You seem to, but I feel better when I've said the magic words.'

'I'll call,' I said, and ducked out the door.

My parents try to keep calm about my nocturnal rambles in the big city, but they do like to know if I am someplace in particular or in limbo out there in the New York subway system. If the latter, only a certain amount of time can elapse before they start having unpleasant fantasies. Since I am small, white and a natural victim, their concern is understandable. I even share it. On the other hand, there is not much any of us can do when I am between places. To limit the period they spend in suspense, I have agreed to make a quick call whenever I start out, but sometimes I forget until I'm part way home. It can go something like this:

'Hello, Mum? It's me, Steve. I'm at Coney Island. I'll be right home.'

'You're where?'

'Look, I took the wrong train. It's too complicated to explain. There should be an F train along in an hour or so. Then I'll change somewhere and be right home.'

'Steve, you have to change at . . . at . . . I'll get my map.'

'Mum, I'll figure it out. Goodbye.'

'Well, thanks for calling, dear. It's always nice to hear your voice from the outposts of civilization.'

'Bye, see you.'

'Bye, dear.'

My mother is a heroine. She burns the candle in the window and tries not to bite her lip too hard. I do what I can to keep her cool.

I felt positively buoyant as I waited for the A train to come and take me the few stops to Dorc's part of town. It was not only the prospect of company which lifted my spirits, it was also my unfailing delight in the unique living space I was about to visit. Dorc's parents were artists, and they lived in a loft way over near the Hudson River south of Canal Street, a desolate area which was only just beginning to be discovered by those of the gentry with strong nerves and an eye to future profits. The Feltrinellis were not gentry. They had lived in their colossal quarters for years and converted them into something quite different from the chic artist's lofts in SoHo or Chelsea. Most notably, these years had allowed time for the plants, of which they were excessively fond, to grow to alarming proportions. Dorc's friends referred to his home as 'the jungle', and in this there was no element of hyperbole. Trees loomed on every side, many of them festooned with vigorous vines and creepers. Carnivorous-looking flowers lurked in the corners. As if this were not enough, five assorted monkeys and a huge red parrot with a terrible voice enjoyed the freedom of the upper branches. Except for the air, which was on the humid side, it was a stimulating place to be.

Dorc, having been born in this curious place, took it for granted. He had a room of his own which we called 'the cube', since that is exactly what it was. Like many loft dwellers, his parents had solved the problem of privacy by throwing up four plywood walls in one corner. It had no windows, but it was all his own. When he felt claustrophobic, he could take a stroll in the jungle. The rest of the time the cube insulated him from his parents, who were both quite mad.

Occupied by these pleasant expectations, I waited for the subway, boarded it and rode the three stops to Canal Street without incident. The A train is often the scene of one or more of New York's little dramas, but it was early still, and no one tried to take my sneakers at knife point or attempted to set fire to some fellow passenger who had been drenched in lighter fluid.

Dorc's mother opened the door to the loft. She was liberally daubed with paint and wore a saffron yellow sari which had clearly not been wound by a practiced hand. Her pale blonde hair had been drawn back in the style favored by Indian matrons, and there was a caste mark peeping out between the patches of red and green on her forehead. Sylvia Feltrinelli was of Swedish origin, but she had her Indian days, her African days, her Japanese days and so on. She greeted me silently with joined palms and a small bow.

'Hari Krishna, hari, hari,' I said, unable on the spur of the moment to think of a more appropriate greeting. 'Is Dorc in the cube?'

'He should be,' Sylvia answered prosaically. 'Why don't you go and see?'

As I drifted toward the cube, I glanced around in the shrubbery hoping to see Dorc's father. We all liked 'the father figure', as Dorc called him. He was, I suppose, as eccentric as his wife, but his was a creative eccentricity, which manifested itself in all kinds of wonderful inventions and works of art. I was especially fond of his mobiles – airy constructs of abstract elegance, born out of the trash cans of lower Manhattan. Large samples of his work rotated peacefully in the spaces between the trees. He was also a designer of stage lighting, and for this craft the jungle was an ideal practice ground. Huge spotlights nestled among the leaves, and heavy cables snaked down between the vines and ran to a sophisticated little switchboard, where Giorgio Feltrinelli played endless games with the atmosphere of his home. His whims were independent of the time of day, so you never knew whether it was going to be noon on the forest floor, with great pools of yellow light beneath the trees, or almost dark, with just a few chilly beams pouring down through the branches. You might also find yourself in a fantasy world where everything had turned purple or gold or deep magenta. The animals seemed to have adapted to these random changes. One would think they might be pretty schizo, but no; they had learned to live with it like the rest of the family.

Having failed to find Giorgio, I pounded on the door of the cube and heard Dorc's languid voice from the other side. 'Enter quietly,' it said, and I obeyed.

To my surprise and slight chagrin, I found my friend no longer expiring from loneliness. Sonia had arrived after all and was sitting folded up in one of her improbable grasshopper poses on the end of Dorc's bed. She was wearing jeans and a hot pink shirt with a disturbing neckline, and her amazing mane of black hair tumbled loose down her back. I regarded the two of them warily, but Sonia, at least, seemed glad to see me.

'It's my favorite hobbit,' she cried. 'Come sit beside me. We have to cheer Dorc up.'

'Hey, Sonia,' I said. 'I thought you were missing.'

'I was on the subway,' she explained, 'for hours and hours and hours.'

'Well, Dorc put out an SOS and here I am, only to find that the cavalry has arrived before me,' I said, still feeling a bit disgruntled.

Dorc stretched his long body in the swivel chair in front of his drawing board. In spite of Sonia's vibrant presence, his patrician features still reflected an apparently overwhelming ennui. This was almost certainly an act.

'Why, one wonders, couldn't your mother have said you were coming?' he asked.

Sonia chortled. 'Because she didn't know, of course. She thought I was going to Pilar's house to spend the night. My God, it was hard enough getting out at all. Carlos was home and feeling protective. He doesn't like me coming down into gringo land at night.'

'Who would?' I said, suppressing a shudder at the thought of the subway between here and East 110th Street.

'I will not be a prisoner, if I can help it,' Sonia said. 'They will have to lock me up and eat the key.'

'You did well,' Dorc said soothingly, 'but what happens when they find out?'

'Lots of shrieking,' Sonia said, 'but who cares? A few screams never hurt anyone, and Carlos isn't home that much. He's the only one I worry about.'

Carlos was Sonia's older brother and to me, at least, an almost mythic figure. He was the idol of the Spanish graffiti writers and engaged in a lot of other colorful activities of marginal legality. Sonia regarded him with a mixture of exasperation and respect. Her parents were seemingly too busy or too confused by the complexity of New York life to keep her in line; but Carlos took big-brotherhood seriously.

I plunked myself on the bed next to Sonia. There were few places to sit in the cube, so the next arrival would get the floor.

'Did I say you could sit down?' Dorc inquired. I threw a pillow at him, and he threw it back. The next shot hit Sonia who returned it with enthusiasm. Feathers were beginning to fill the air, and all of us had cheered up enormously when the phone rang. Dorc answered it and listened a moment. Then, 'Come,' he said and hung up. 'That was Will,' he added for our benefit. 'He's just had a Chicken McNuggets over on Broadway and is coming here for first aid. I wonder where I put the stomach pump.'

'Good,' I said, pleased at the thought; another male would make me feel less of a fifth wheel. 'How did he sound – apart from being sick?'

'Portentous; judicial; pregnant with plans,' Dorc said.

Sonia giggled. 'I love Will when he gets that way,' she said. 'He sounds just like his father, which is about the last thing he would want.' (Will's father was a judge – a black judge, if you can imagine anything so oppressively respectable.)

'Poor Will,' I said. 'He'll never lose that dignified

manner, no matter how hard he tries. He must have learned it in the cradle.'

'What do you suppose tonight's costume will be?' Sonia mused.

'Something none of the rest of us could have found if we'd looked a hundred years,' Dorc said.

I sighed enviously. 'Something none of the rest of us could wear either.' Will had a genius for costumes, all of which looked fantastic on his six feet plus of ebony elegance. I was a master of disguise myself, but felt my unprepossessing form could only run to the whimsical or, at times, the downright disreputable.

Since it is not far from the McDonalds on lower Broadway to the loft, our curiosity was soon satisfied. Will arrived and filled the tiny room with his overwhelming presence. He was wearing a three-piece suit of forest-green, a candy-striped shirt, and a bowler hat.

'Will, darling,' Sonia gasped. 'I want it. Where did you get it?'

Will raised an enormous hand. 'Greetings, friends. You like the latest? It comes, of course, from my usual boutique at Forty-sixth and Tenth Avenue. You've got to go there, Sonia. They have the most amazing dresses – sequins, spangles, satin – you name it, the Salvation Army's got it.'

'Yuck,' Sonia said. 'You wouldn't catch me dead in that place.'

'The social insecurity of the recent immigrant,' Dorc said.

'Shut up, Dorc. I'm not an immigrant, recent or otherwise, and my mother shops there, if you must know.'

'All is explained,' Dorc said, and was rewarded with a venomous look.

Will meanwhile had shed his jacket and folded up on the floor, most of which he occupied. 'Remind me to come early for a good seat next time,' he said. 'Well, now that we're all here and no one can move, what shall we do?'

'I can reach the radio,' Dorc suggested.

'Yes, but why?' I asked. 'There's nothing on but disco.' (We all liked rock and hated disco – a distinction which seemed fuzzy to our parents, but which divided our generation into two, often literally, warring camps.)

'Anyway, we can't just sit and listen to music,' Sonia said. 'Think of something.'

'Not me,' Dorc said. 'I summoned you all here to amuse me, and I'm still waiting.'

'We need to do a new graffiti piece,' Will said. 'One splendid effort is not enough. We're stagnating.'

'One piece won't make us famous,' I said, 'but it's still a great thing. I checked it out the other day, and it's still there, in all its astonishing, psychedelic technicolor.'

'Man, nothing is going to happen to that piece,' Will said. 'At least not until they tear the building down which, now that I think of it, probably won't be long. On the other hand, nobody is going to see it either except a bunch of winos, and they probably think it's just a normal part of the scenery. Hell, they see things like that all the time, and a lot of the graphics they view are *animated*.'

A few weeks ago the four of us had done a big graffiti piece on a wall just off the Bowery. That a group of so-called middle-class kids should want to do such a thing may seem strange; but it is fairly common, especially among art students. We are not so mad at the world as the ghetto kids, but we share their love of excitement and of screwing the system one way or another. And since we are artists, the adornment of public places with big, colorful letters has a natural appeal. As to leaving our names all over the city of New York, I guess a lot of people who wouldn't do it can still understand it if they try. The life of a New York public-high-school student is somewhat downtrodden and anonymous at best. Who doesn't want to make his mark on the face of the world?

Our problem was that we were all too chicken to go to the train yards and fight it out with the big graffiti artists for the right to do a subway car. We were also scared stiff of the law. Nobody wants to get caught, but maybe with our backgrounds we didn't want to get caught even more than most. This left us with very little scope for our talents. We could spend our time tagging, which did begin to pall after a while; or we could practise spray painting on the unappealing surface of some building nobody cared enough about to guard.

Finally we had found this one good wall. It was big and the surface was not too bad. Even more remarkably, it was still innocent of graffiti. This was hard to explain since those infantile scribblers known as 'toys' in New York graffiti jargon are completely unable to pass up any blank surface anywhere. They are responsible for most of the mess that people get so excited about, and they give the rest of us a bad name. None of them would know a piece of art if it came up and bit him in the ass. But they had missed our wall somehow, and for that we were duly grateful. We were also pleased with the lighting, a dim glow which spread around the corner of the building from a street light halfway down the block. It was enough to see by, but only just. You don't want to work on a graffiti piece in a goldfish bowl. Nobody seemed to care what happened to this lovely wall, and the only stares we got were from the Bowery bums who, as Will said, probably thought the giant letters that flowed from our spray cans were just part of another boozy dream.

Following a rough sketch we had made in the loft, we put our four names in a square with a border of smoke and flames swirling around the outside. Dorc used his own nickname, because it was short and already sounded like a tag. Sonia had chosen 'Astra' for reasons best known to herself, and Will called himself 'Toad' or 'Mr Toad' or sometimes, in an extravagant moment, 'Toad of Toad Hall'. (When I hadn't known Will very long, I asked him why he had picked this bizarre tag. He looked down at me with his slow, mocking smile and said, 'Because I like fast cars and big houses, white boy.' I understood the allusion, but not until much later did I understand the fun Will got out of this kind of put-on. It was meant to confuse his numerous white friends, and it did – at least for a while.)

Anyway, in the end we were well pleased with our first big piece, and we had gotten a lot of badly needed practice with spray paint in the process. The big question now seemed to be, Whither the gang of four? Would we go on to greater glory? Or would we have to go back to tagging the posts in empty subway stations with our distinctive but still far from famous names?

'I still say we have to go to the yards,' Sonia said. 'I may not want to go, and I sure know better than you pampered darlings what it's like out there, but that's where the scene is. That's where it's happening. The only pieces that are worth anything are being done on the trains, and the only place you can work on the trains is out there.' She swept one long arm in a circle to suggest the horrible outer reaches of Brooklyn, Queens and the Bronx.

'They only get buffed,' I said, hoping to divert attention from my basic cowardice.

Dorc sighed. 'Art is ephemeral,' he said, 'but I, personally, would prefer not to be. Putting this group in the subway yards is like sending the future of American art on a kamikaze mission.'

'Bull crap, Dorc. That's just a fancy way of saying you're scared out of your mind,' Will said.

'And you're not, I suppose?'

'Not of the toys, I'm not,' Will said, 'or even of the big gangs. But when it comes to the forces of law and order, personified by a certain very heavy judge – that, my friends, is a different story. Getting caught in the train yards with a spray can in my hand would be the final blow to this father-son relationship, believe me.'

'It would be hairy,' I agreed, 'but wouldn't your dad spring you if you got busted? He's in such a good position to do it.' (I knew my father would, of course, if he possibly could. This was one advantage I had over the others. I knew what my parents would do in some dire emergency. So, apparently, did Will, but the outlook there wasn't so good. My naive question was treated with the derision it deserved.)

'Man, you have got to be smarter than that. You have heard all about the judge. You have even met the judge. And you can sit right there and ask if he would get me out of the slammer once I had broken the law?'

It was true. I remembered all too well the first and last time the fierce, judicial gaze of Judge Conrad had rested upon my insignificant person – my frayed, purple Adidas, my black band-jacket with the red piping, the somewhat pornographic art gallery of buttons displayed across my chest. It was not a moment either of us cared to repeat.

'The first thing he would do,' Will continued, 'would be to decide whether my disgrace was enough of a story to hit the papers – "Judge's Son Jailed for Graffiti" –

that sort of thing. Then he would make a statement, either to the press or to my captors.' Will's voice deepened dramatically. '"Gentlemen, if my son has broken the ordinances of this city, he must pay whatever penalty the law requires." Then he would go home and forget all about me.'

'I bet he wouldn't,' I said bravely. 'Forget, I mean.'

'What the hell do you know about it?' Will shouted. He wasn't kidding around any more.

'Hey man, sorry. Cool it. I don't know anything about it,' I mumbled.

'Then keep your stupid mouth shut,' Will said, and subsided like a volcano, quiet for the moment but still, I thought, seething underneath.

Sonia and Dorc had been watching this exchange with the avid interest of spectators at a bullfight. Now that it seemed that no real blood was going to flow, they were ready to go back to the original problem.

'All this isn't getting us any new and wonderful graffiti spaces,' Dorc said. 'You know how Steve and I feel about going to the yards. We're just not cut out for it. Will feels the same way for different reasons. And you, chick, are also in total agreement only you don't want to admit it.'

'Don't call me chick, you pig,' Sonia retorted. But this was just a reflex. If Dorc had hoped to get a feminist battle going, he was going to be disappointed for once. Sonia was thinking through her position, and it was more complicated than ours.

'You know how much I want to score off Carlos,' she said. 'But getting us all mangled would definitely not produce the right effect. He'd pick up the pieces, kill whoever had laid a hand on his precious sister, and then he would give two lectures, one to you guys about staying in the little league, where you belong, and one to me about staying home and developing my talent for china painting. But I don't have any talents for china painting, or for greeting cards or for nice, folksy pictures of Hispanic families playing checkers on the stoop. I'm a graffiti artist, and I'm as good as he is.' Sonia paused for breath, her black eyes flashing. Then she said in a small voice, 'I'm better than he is actually, or I would be, if I could get any practice. And he knows it.'

'But that isn't why he wants to keep you wrapped up in cotton wool,' Dorc said.

Sonia looked at him miserably. 'No, it's not the only reason, anyway. It's not that simple. Nothing ever is.'

'He wants to keep you safe,' I said, with my gift for always saying the wrong thing. 'He thinks you're fantastic, and he doesn't want anything to happen to you.'

'And you can say that again and again and again,' Sonia said bitterly. 'I mean he doesn't want *anything* to happen to me, *ever*, until some handsome *caballero* comes along and puts a ring on my finger. Then I can start having babies, and the jerk with the ring can go back to messing around with all his old girlfriends, and life can go on repeating itself like a broken record. Well, I'm not buying it. I'm going to show those bastards and show them good. How, when and where are the only questions.'

'Oh, well, as to those little problems . . .' Dorc said with an airy gesture.

'And isn't this just where we all came in?' Will added. He seemed to have forgotten his own grievances during Sonia's recital of hers.

'How, when and where,' Dorc repeated. 'Of which "where" is the only really interesting item. Presumably once the "where" is settled, the "how" and "when" can be worked out.'

There was a long silence, during which Dorc turned to his drawing table and took out a big sheet of white paper.

He began to write swiftly with a calligraphy pen. He was the only one of us who had ever really liked the lettering sections of our art courses. The following list, in a variety of elegant calligraphic styles, is what he finally produced:

DESCRIPTION OF A PERFECT (OR AT LEAST ACCEPTABLE) GRAFFITI SPACE

THIS SPACE MUST BE:

1. Highly visible to a number of people who are
   a. not totally soused
   b. not hopelessly stupid
   c. maybe even a little bit informed about graffiti
2. Not immediately liable to destruction (although we realize this is asking too much)
3. Possible to work on in terms of
   a. accessibility, i.e., not the piers of the Brooklyn Bridge or a frieze around the top of one of the World Trade Center towers
   b. reasonably good surface
   c. light – some but not too much for a night project
   d. fair odds against interruption by the forces of law and order or other concerned citizens, hostile or merely interfering
4. Safe for the artists involved (see 3d, above)

By the time Dorc had finished, we had all had a look at his list and sat down again.

'I don't see what good that does,' Sonia said.

'It always helps to get your head in order,' Dorc replied. 'Then the good, wacky ideas can start to flow.'

'It just dams them up, if you ask me. A list like that freezes my brain solid.' Sonia seemed irritable and argumentative, but then we were all on edge. Too little had happened for too long.

Meanwhile, something was teasing at the edge of my mind. I shook my head angrily, as if it were a bee around my ears, but like a bee, this only made it more persistent. I got up and hit my head gently three or four times on the wall of the cube, which only distracted me briefly and the others not at all. By now I had their undivided attention, though for once I could have lived without it.

'Out with it, man,' Will said.

'It's nothing, really. Just a passing thought.' There was a skeptical silence, and I knew I was the one who was going to have to break it. Finally I said, reluctantly, and without my usual amazing eloquence, 'Well, I saw this old World War II movie a while ago – about pilots, you know, bomber pilots and these big old crates they flew and how they got sort of, that is, really *very* attached to their planes and gave them names and, well, and all that . . .'

'And painted all over them,' Sonia cried. 'Yeah, sometimes just the nose or the door, but sometimes the whole plane got covered with all sorts of things – girls and flowers and names and bursting bombs – whatever the men felt like. They never got buffed either. They flew on and on as long as they didn't get shot down. Everybody on the ground knew the planes and crews by their graffiti. They'd watch them come in out of the clouds with their nude girls or their flying cows or their messages for Hitler or Hirohito. Except that they were legal, they were the greatest graffiti ever.' She was on her feet by now, and I was appalled to see how taken she was with my dubious idea.

Will was giving me and Sonia the look we deserved, the gentle, wary, pitying look we keep for those who are truly, but we hope harmlessly, around the bend. 'Sonia, my dear, sit down and use those excellent feminine brain cells. Steve, you feel all right now, my little man?'

'You asked for it,' I snapped. 'I can't help what runs through my mind. If you hadn't insisted, wild wallabies wouldn't have dragged it out of me.'

'Not true,' Dorc said. 'Once an idea like that gets born, it never dies unless you pull it out on the floor and stamp on it, and sometimes it even survives stamping. Let's go play some pinball.'

'Do what?' I asked.

'This kind of thing needs to be swamped under a wave of meaningless, brain-washing, stupid activity. Then if it comes back, we have to give it another chance. We can hope it will die of neglect.'

'You can't be serious,' Will said.

'No, let's think about it now,' Sonia begged. 'It's fantastic. It's absolutely the wildest thing I ever heard of. It's . . .'

'The product of a disordered mind,' Will finished. 'I'm with brother Dorc. What we need right now is to act normal for a while, and maybe it will all go away.'

'Pinball and beer,' Dorc said firmly. He sprang to his feet and led the way out past the refrigerator and into the bosky dell at one end of the loft, in which the father figure had built a truly incredible pinball machine. Giorgio had a particularly bad case of Tolkien-mania which burst forth from time to time in unexpected places. Here it found expression in a kind of pinball fantasia. On this machine, instead of following the usual banal course, the little ball plunged through the hazardous wilds of Middle Earth. Here it skirted a pack of orcs and there it barely missed entanglement in the spider webs of Mirkwood. At the end, of course, there was a gleaming dragon horde and an elfin princess, fair beyond the dreams of mortal man. It was all painted in the most fantastic colors, and the lights that flashed and the noises it made were also right out of this world. Add to these joys the age-old fascination of the game, and you can see how we soon forgot our previous problems.

After about an hour of this healing frivolity, I began to have the nagging feeling that my family might be thinking evil thoughts concerning my whereabouts. Also I was tired, which does happen occasionally. Sonia and Will had the look of people who have settled in for the night, but nobody suggested that I should find a corner to curl up in, so I headed for the door.

Sonia, of course, was not about to let me get away that easily. She caught my exit out of the corner of her eye and abandoned the ball she was playing to its own devices. 'Steve, wait,' she called. 'You can't go until we've talked about your idea.'

'I disown it,' I said brutally. 'You guys talk about it if you want to, and then it'll be your idea. I'm going home.'

'Go right ahead,' Dorc said, 'but if this thing goes anywhere, don't think anyone is going to forget who started it. For better or for worse, it's your baby.'

In fact, as I discovered later, they didn't talk about the plan again that night, but that doesn't mean we didn't all think about it. You can't forget a thing like that any more than you can forget someone saying he knows a foolproof way to dye the whole school purple.

While I was fishing for my coat in the foyer, Giorgio Feltrinelli materialized from behind a flowering bush. 'How, vartlet!' he cried. 'Slip thee from the fray on stealthy, sneakered feet? Have at you now!' and he lunged at me with a long plastic rod he was carrying. I grabbed an umbrella from among the coats and gave him parry and thrust for a minute. Dorc's father was short and a little stout, but quick. It wasn't long before he had me pinned against the front door.

'Have mercy, good Sir Giorgio,' I said. 'My noble parents are burning their last candle in the tower window. I must be gone.'

'Ah, is it even so,' he sighed. 'And I had a quest of surpassing interest in my mind for you.'

'I fear I must decline, my lord,' I said regretfully. Giorgio's quests were always interesting, but they usually took the better part of the night, so I edged my way out, bowing and scraping. Maybe if I had met him earlier, when I was looking for him, I would never have thought of the plane, and this would have been a different story or no story at all. But that's the way life goes. One thing leads to another and, first thing you know, you're doing something you never would have believed possible.

CHAPTER 2

When the door of the loft closed behind me, I was already in another world. The two long flights of stairs went down between scarred, discolored walls, past the metal doors of the other tenants. Most of these had four or five locks punctuating their battered surfaces. There was a decidedly raunchy picture drawn on the wall next to one of the doors, and I wondered who had done it and why nobody had painted it out. In fact, a few buckets of paint would have done great things for the whole stairwell, but I guess nobody cared. This is something you often see in loft buildings. The entrance and stairs are left in their original, beat-up state, while the lofts themselves – the secret worlds behind the metal doors – brim with light and shine with new paint. Behind those doors are stereo sets with rows of knobs, gourmet kitchens, original paintings, handmade rugs on glowing waxed floors. Outside, the desolation of Smaug. Oh well, I suppose it's one way of getting ready for the street.

Actually, I felt better once I was outside. Even when I'm a bit scared, I am at home in the city streets. This is the New York feeling: a little scared, a little excited, free. A wet, early-spring snow was falling in big flakes that died as soon as they hit the ground. To the right was a vacant lot, with an abandoned dock behind it and then the river. A small light was moving out there in the snow – maybe a freighter slipping quietly away on the black water, leaving New York, as my parents always longed to do. I felt around for my feelings about this while my feet hustled along towards Canal Street. Where was it going out there in the swirling dark? Italy? Greece? Someplace where white houses climbed up out of a blue bay. Someplace where you could sit half the day at a table in a sunny piazza and never feel hassled or nervous. No, I told myself firmly, as I turned the corner away from the river. It's going to Liverpool or Hamburg or maybe even Iceland. It's going someplace even colder and a lot less interesting. My memories of a year in Italy often warred with my conviction that New York was the only place where anything important ever happened. I sighed. There was no point in thinking about it. Someday when I had made twice as many friends as I had now and all my teachers had learned to put up with me, my father would come home all pink with excitement and say, 'Well, Steve, how would you like to live in Timbuctoo?' Then my parents would go on to say that if I really didn't want to go, they would give up this enormously interesting job with its fantastic pay in this marvelous foreign city and stay home. What can I say? It sounds as if I think my parents are hypocrites, but they're really not, except when it comes to foreign travel. They really do want me to be happy, and my mother, at least, has some inkling of what it means to change schools every few minutes. Besides, they have a real problem. In the first place, my father's work does involve a certain amount of dashing around. In the second place, they both really believe that the grass is greener on the other side of the water. Unfortunately (or maybe fortunately), I have some of their wanderlust myself, especially when they wander towards one of the places I've been and liked. But I could still live without this we-won't-go-if-you-don't-want-to bit. That's bull, and they know it.

During the course of these mental meanderings, I had arrived at the Canal Street stop of the A train without thinking too much about what I would do if somebody jumped me in this deserted part of town. A New York subway station at one a.m. is enough to make anyone dream of foreign shores, but I was distracted by a new piece of graffiti on the wall of the stairwell. It was a small but perfect griffin of the sort that I used to do a few years ago. Of course, the style was different. This was an original artist, not the ghost of Steve Wiley at thirteen, and an artist with a very fine, sure line. Underneath he had written the words 'Griffin Man'. While I was admiring the drawing and feeling twinges of nostalgia for my old mythological days, I was also thinking that this kid shouldn't lock himself into a tag that no one but a freak like me would appreciate. Why was I so sure that the unknown writer was very young? It was the subject matter, wasn't it? Certainly the execution was mature. A nasty doubt stirred in my mind. Maybe somewhere out there was a big dude, older than me, equally or *more* accomplished, who was so cool he could have drawn fairies dancing around a toadstool ring without worrying about his image.

I shook myself. All this was just late-night moonshine, like my thoughts about the ship on the river. But I still wanted to know who had drawn the griffin. I took out my marker and wrote carefully under the tag, 'Griffin Man, Call the Troll King, (718) 789–4089.' That wasn't very original and certainly no tag I had ever used, but it was simple and easy to remember. At my end, if someone called and asked for the Troll King, my mother would have no trouble figuring out who was wanted. She has taken calls for aardvark counseling, werewolf therapy and many other oddities, without faltering. She can do it in her sleep, but it's better if she doesn't have to.

I called home from the platform. Don't ask me why I never call from a friend's house. I just don't like to, that's all. My mother answered with a promptness which made me suspect that she had been lying on the phone.

'Hi, it's me. I'm in the station.'

'Which station, Steve?'

'Canal Street A train.'

'Fantastic. See you soon, then.'

'If the train comes soon, you'll see me soon,' I said philosophically, and hung up.

It was, of course, a long wait, and while it lasted my mind strayed inevitably back to my vision of World War II bombers covered with graffiti. From there it was a short step to the thought of some vast, intercontinental jumbo jet glowing from nose to tail with glorious, swirling colors. 'That is one cosmically beautiful idea,' I said aloud to the empty station. And then, 'Please come, train, before I start seeing pink elephants.' Eventually it came, but not before I had started in on the design for my own section. Up around the door it would be, where a lot of people would see it. I would incorporate the door into the design so that even when it was open . . . 'Madness!' I shouted to the big A as it came roaring down the track.

CHAPTER 3

Our apartment was dim and deeply peaceful. The recessed ceiling lights were turned down to a soft, rosy glow, and just a tiny tongue of flame ran along the charred log in the fireplace. Sometimes I thought living on the fourth floor of a house in Brooklyn was a pain, and sometimes I thought it couldn't be more perfect. Tonight was one of the perfect times. The city and the subway might have been on another planet. The door to my parents' room was open, so I went in. By the light from the living room I could see two yellow eyes and two pointed, black ears, silhouetted against the pale comforter. The rest of Nero was a long shadow squeezed between my parents' legs. My mother lifted her head from the cave of Dad's shoulder. 'Hi, love. Glad you're back,' she said softly.

'Hi, Mum. Wake me at seven.'

'Tomorrow's not a school day,' she protested.

'I know it's not, but I've got lots to do,' I said. 'OK? Sleep tight.'

She subsided with a whimper. My mother was convinced that I was burning myself out, in spite of all evidence to the contrary. She loved to sleep. So did I, to tell the truth, but it seemed like such a waste of time.

Then, too, she knew and I knew that half the time I chickened out on these early risings and slept on well past my parents, sometimes even as late as noon. Those were the times when I caught up on all the other times. It worked fine, and someday she was going to get around to buying an extra alarm clock and turning the whole problem over to me.

In my own room, I turned on the lamp over my drafting table. This was a mistake, since my eye immediately lighted on a half-finished drawing. In an instant I saw where it had to go next. I sat down and chose a good pen. The seven o'clock rising was doomed unless I worked all night, in which case some other part of the day would probably go down the drain – probably but not certainly; it depended on what turned up. I reached over and switched the radio on low. Now the night was all mine, a private world of time within the private world of the apartment. Huge circles of delicious loneliness seemed to expand from the small center where I sat. They were like gentle waves pushing the outside world farther and farther away. I started to work on the drawing slowly, contentedly. After all, I had all night.

CHAPTER 4

It was more than a week before the four of us got together again. During this time the weather continued to be disagreeable, which got on everyone's nerves. Our teachers manifested their misery in surprise quizzes on subjects no one had ever heard of. All the art classes turned with new vigor to the well-worn subject of gothic lettering. The student body responded with guerilla diversions just short of open warfare. It was the February syndrome extended into late March, and everyone felt cheated and abused.

Dorc and I had been in the same art section for two semesters. This was a minor miracle, since the bureaucratic machinery of the school usually succeeded in preventing anyone from knowing anyone else for more than about four months. At the end of each semester a sort of volcanic eruption occurred, during which 2,000 students, who had begun to find cozy social niches, suddenly found themselves thrown up in the air and dropped into the laps of new teachers among classes of total strangers. I had been assured when I entered the school that the chances of ever again finding anyone I liked after such an upheaval were vanishingly small. Perhaps this system was designed to prevent revolutionary cadres from forming, but I suspect that, like so many other unpleasant things, it was just an accident of bureaucracy. Of course, we saw each other in the cafeteria at lunch time, along with a lot of other people with strong stomachs. We also met there before school started and sat around rapping and drawing on our pads. If you wanted to have any kind of social life and see friends from other classes, you had to get up disgustingly early.

Anyway, Dorc and I sat next to each other for a whole year in art which, I sometimes thought, was the only thing that made life tolerable. On this particular day, even he had had enough of lettering. He looked up from a page of big, black letters adorned with obscene, crawling things in pink and green. 'Something must be done to brighten this dreary existence,' he said in a fairly loud voice – loud enough, that is, to reach me over the grumbling of the rest of the class.

Mr Weinberg gave us an only moderately hostile stare. After all, we weren't throwing things or dismantling the furniture, and besides, we were his prize students.

'Yes, but what?' I said. 'I've been trying to think of something, but my brain hurts.'

'Another graffiti meeting,' Dorc answered. 'And then we've got to do something together – anything, just to get moving and prove that we're alive.'

'In this weather?' I said, looking towards the window. Amazingly a large patch of blue shone behind its grimy glass. 'Hey, look at that. You're right. Let's see if we can find the others and meet at the pits after school.' ('The pits' was The Burger Pit around the corner from school. It came by its nickname in several logical ways, but it did have big, gloomy booths with high backs, where one could be reasonably sure of privacy.)

Dorc agreed, and it remained only to find Will and

Sonia in the milling herd after school. To an outsider this might seem impossible. They were both tall, but in a place where only shortness stood out. The damn school was full of basketball players, male and female. We had, however, almost instant success. You get an instinct for where your friends will be in a New York high school.

When the four of us reached the sidewalk, we found that the sky really was clearing, and a sweet wind was blowing up the river from the south.

'Spring!' Sonia cried. 'Spring, spring, spring! I can't believe it.' She threw her arms around me and lifted me off the ground.

'Hey, Sonia. Don't do that, do you mind?' I said when she had put me down.

'But I'm so happy, and I love you, Stevie. You're like my little brother. I don't have a little brother. All I've got is big, mean Carlos, and I sure can't pick him up and twirl him around.' She giggled delightedly at the idea.

'Maybe I don't want to be your little brother,' I said sourly. 'Had you thought of that?'

Sonia had the wit to look contrite. 'I'm sorry, Steve,' she said. 'I can't help it if I'm a bean-pole. All the Spanish girls seem to be shooting up like this.'

'And all the black girls, and all the white girls, and even all the damned Oriental girls,' I said. But I wasn't really pissed off. The sun was too warm, the wind too promising; and here were the four of us headed for a conference of huge importance at the pits. 'You wait, girl,' I said, drawing myself up to my full five feet three inches. 'I am about to experience the famous adolescent growth spurt, and then beware, all ye tall and slender maidens.'

'I can't wait,' Sonia said agreeably, and she took my arm as we swung after Will and Dorc through the door of our favorite haunt.

'Cosmic funkiness,' I said, as I saw them heading for the last booth. The last booth was unpopular since it was right off the kitchen and often smelled of rancid cat liver, but this unpleasantness was offset by its extreme gloom and comparative isolation. Once entrenched in its cheerless depths, we were fairly safe from the approaches of our fellow students. Sleazy Susie took our modest orders, and we eased into conversation through the usual channel of bitching about school.

'I'm going to kill the Finkelman,' Dorc said. 'You are all cordially invited to her complete, slow dismemberment. She gave a surprise quiz today on a unit we hadn't even started. Everyone bombed; even Liz the Whiz, which was some consolation. But what does the silly bitch think she's doing?'

'She was undoubtedly sloshed, poor lady,' Will said. 'You can't blame her. It's a case of diminished responsibility.'

'Man, those grades go in the book even if they're soaked in gin,' Dorc said. 'And what am I supposed to say to college admissions? "Oh please, sir. Do disregard my chemistry grade. My teacher was a lush, you see, and seldom knew what she was doing."' (In spite of, or perhaps because of, his weird upbringing, Dorc was hell-bent on the Ivy League.)

'Somebody should report her,' Sonia said. 'Somebody's parent, maybe?' She was looking hopefully at me and Will.

'No, I wouldn't do that,' I said regretfully. 'And neither would my parents. The poor broad might lose her job. Besides, she's not the only one. If they started clearing out the teachers who take something for their nerves, the place would have to close down.'

'Cosmic,' Sonia said.

'Cosmic catastrophe,' I replied. 'You'd be back in your old high school, which is all right, I guess, if you really dig no art, third-grade readers and being knifed every other day. Will would be sent away to be the token nigger in some New England boarding school. My parents would keep me home with a shiny new library card and no chance to see anybody. I don't know what horrors would be in store for Dorc if the dear old commercial-artist assembly-line closed down, but let's take no chances.'

'Probably close anyway with all the city budget cuts,' Will said gloomily. 'I guess we should be glad we've still got teachers, whatever their condition.'

'They seem to try,' Dorc said. 'Some of them, anyway. Miss Guernsey tries.'

'Moo,' we all responded in unison.

'And another thing,' Dorc continued. 'Why can't teachers have reasonable names? Finkelman, Guernsey, Nixon. One way or another that's just asking for it. All teachers upon entering a school system should be given neutral names, like Smith or Jones.'

'So they can be called Smitty and Jonesy?' Sonia said. 'You, of all people, ought to know how tricky it is to avoid nicknames.'

'It may be tricky,' Dorc replied, 'but if you're thinking of my sad case, as you obviously are, it should be clear that the elder Feltrinellis didn't even try. A great wave of respectability washed over them when they found they had done something so bourgeois as to produce a son, and Dorsey was the grim result.'

'It could have been worse,' I said with relish, fully prepared to elaborate on the theme.

Dorc was ahead of me. 'Obviously,' he said. 'They could have been into Norse mythology or Greek drama or Haitian voodoo. Let your mind roam over the grisly possibilities sometime, when you're sitting on a dead subway car in the middle of a tunnel and you've read all the legible tags twice and are starting in on the ones that seem to have been written by a crazed elephant with a marker in its trunk. I often do.'

'Do what?' I asked. 'I got lost back thar 'round the bend.'

'He broods about what his parents might have named him in one of their wilder moments,' Sonia explained. 'Now speaking of graffiti . . .'

'Were we?' Will asked.

'Speaking of graffiti,' Sonia continued firmly, 'where are we going to do that big piece? Personally, I can't get Steve's idea out of my head.'

'My idea? Did I have an idea? Oh, super cool. Was it any good? I'll bet it was wowsers, if I can only remember what it was.'

'Shut up, Steve. You're babbling,' Will said, 'and you don't fool these smart cats for one small minute. There's a great, long, silvery jet plane right here in everybody's head, the only problem being it has four different things painted on its great big beautiful belly.'

'Belly?' Dorc said. 'I thought maybe the wings . . .' He trailed off.

'Around the windows,' Sonia said.

'Too hard to reach,' I objected.

Will held up a huge, dark paw. 'You see what I mean? I'm sure you do. So let's take the last contribution first, in view of its slightly intelligent, negative character. "Too hard to reach," he says, and there in a nutshell is the problem. Man, the whole thing is too hard to reach. It's too high up and too far out, and above all, too well guarded to reach. You don't just go out to an airport when it gets dark and start spray-painting a plane, hoping nobody will notice.'

'Oh, don't shoot it down before it's even had a chance to fly,' Sonia said. 'What's the matter with you guys? If no one ever dreams of doing anything new, everything stays just the same. The same boring old world just goes on and on. We think we're pretty good, don't we, and different and special. Oh yes we do. We don't bomb trains and we don't scribble on statues, and we're scared to go to the yards, but we're graffiti artists all the same, and if we give up on a cool idea just because it's a little impractical, we might as well be dead.'

'Girl, you take my breath away. You absolutely do,' Will said, but you could tell he was impressed. Will's problem was that being the oldest, and having that judge for a father, he felt he had to be sensible and keep some sort of lid on the rest of us. In fact, he was the most innovative artist I had ever met, and he had the balls, too once he'd decided something was worth doing, to do it no matter what. There isn't anyone I'd rather have around in a crunch situation, and not just because he's big and black. So we never paid too much attention to his fatherly pronouncements. They were partly 'for the record' and partly his way of thinking things through ahead of time.

'So let's rap about it,' Dorc said impatiently. 'It can't do any harm.'

I had thought it over more than I cared to admit, so now I took the plunge. 'It may not be totally impossible,' I said. 'I mean, it's nearly impossible, but if we're going to think about it at all, we have to say, "Well, hey, harder things have been done," and go on from there. I mean, look at all the amazingly hard things that have been done. Look at prison breaks, just for example. I read a book once about this totally secure prison in Nazi Germany where they put all the really brilliant prisoners – the ones who had gotten out of all the other places but hadn't made it over the border. This place was so secure even the cockroaches were wearing stripes. Man, it had everything: cliffs, moats, dogs, hundreds of guards, all the best gadgets. So, of course, it wasn't long before these ingenious dudes started leaking out. They didn't all get away, but a lot of them did. And the point is they got their ideas by sitting down and rapping about how you could do an impossible thing.'

'Brainstorming,' Dorc said. 'That's what it's called. But first let's make sure we know what we want to do and that we all want more or less the same thing.'

'But that's obvious,' Sonia said.

'I'd like it to be a little more obvious,' Dorc answered. 'We've all been doing it in our heads. Now let's go beyond the simple idea that a big plane would make a real cool graffiti space. Its appeal is obvious, I'll grant you that. A plane is transportation which puts it in the same tradition as the trains, but with a fantastic difference, right? And it's big, and it's got terrific visibility.'

'And the powers-that-be would wet their collective pants,' Will added with relish.

'Absolutely,' Dorc said. 'Now, let's move another square. Take visibility – impact on the public. Who is going to see this amazing creation, assuming we get it done and depart with our skins intact? Who will be the viewers who look and gasp and yell, "Horrible!" or "Beautiful!" or "How the hell did those damn kids do that?" Surely not just a handful of dull-eyed airport workers?'

'Come on, Dorc,' I said. 'The people who are going to get on the plane, of course, and a lot of other people who are taking other planes nearby or meeting friends or seeing them off. Hordes of people, I should think. And then there will be all the others we can only guess at – the ones at the other end, wherever it's going.' Something had made my heart start pounding. 'London!' I shouted. 'Paris, Rome, Athens, Berlin. Moscow, Peking, Tokyo, Singapore!'

'Not all on one flight, cretin,' Dorc said witheringly.

'No, but we should get one that goes as many places as possible.'

'A message from New York,' Sonia said in an awed voice.

For a moment we were silent, contemplating the sheer magnificence of our vision – a giant plane, blazing with our colors, zooming in to land at great cities all over the world. It would be the statement to end all statements. Probably none of us would ever bother to write our names on a subway car again; or maybe we would, just so people would know someone famous had passed that way. Because famous we would surely be – famous or infamous or probably both. I sighed, and Will looked at me.

'Dreams of glory, little brother? Yeah, me too, I guess. A graffiti message from New York. That's chilly, that is. Should it say something, I wonder, or just have our names done in our most inimitable styles?'

'Names are enough,' Dorc said. 'A big piece is a statement in itself.'

'But not so much to people in other countries,' I said. 'At least, in Italy they aren't hung up on spreading their names around the way we are, and they don't do art graffiti so much. Even when they do, there's always a political message too. It's a national habit. The little kids choose up sides when they're about five years old and start writing "friggin' fascists", or "communist pigs" all over everything, with their first crayolas.'

'But if it's a message, it has to be a message everyone

can dig,' Sonia said. 'Something like "love" or "peace", some one word that turns everybody on.'

'Sonia, that is very, very uncool,' Will said, in his most repressive voice.

But Sonia was not about to be put down. She had an inspired look which made her really beautiful. Her big, black eyes were wide open, as if she'd just seen a heavenly vision, and she wasn't talking fast or jumping up and down the way she usually does when a great idea hits her. She spoke quietly, and we all listened. 'Don't anybody give me "uncool" or "corny" or any of those words. That's kid stuff. That's for people who are afraid to say anything serious for fear someone will make fun of them – for fear somebody will think they really care about something. But we've got to be better than that. Maybe "love" is a tricky word. I sort of agree that it's been spoiled. It's nice, but it's got a mushy sound. But "peace" is different. It's still pure. No matter how many messed up people use it for a catchword or a greeting or a slogan, it still sounds like what it means. "*Paz*",' she finished softly. 'It's simple. It's something everybody wants.'

'*Pace*,' I said, not to be outdone in the language department. Now I was having a vision of my own, which was more artistic than moral or political. 'Hey, you know, just from a design angle we ought to get a plane that's going somewhere with a foreign alphabet. Can't you see the same great word not only written in four languages but in four different kinds of writing? Like, Arabic has to be one of them. A word written in Arabic is like an abstract painting – except, I suppose, to an Arab. Anyway, it would be truly cosmic.'

'To bc truly cosmic you'd havc to writc it in Martian,' Dorc said, and I threw my wadded up napkin at him for want of a more deadly missile.

At this point we became aware that Sleazy Susie was standing by our booth and regarding us with her arms folded in a menacing way.

'My dear young lady,' Will said. 'Did you, by any chance, want us to order something over and above the delicious beverages which we consumed with such enthusiasm so long ago?'

'Don't give me none of that fancy talk, you,' Susie said. 'The boss don't give this table away, ya know.'

'He should, but he don't. Shall we have another round, or risk eviction from this choice spot?'

'I'm broke,' I said, and the other two looked equally reluctant.

Will sighed and reached for his wallet, as he so frequently did on these occasions. 'Fill 'em up, sweetheart, and then stop hanging over us like a harpy ready to tear at our vitals.'

'Don't you cheapskates ever eat?' Susie snarled as she gathered up the empty cups and glasses.

We ignored this familiar sally, and Will said, 'I figured we had some more to say, and I can't think with that creature's glittering eyeball bent upon me. Now the problem of what we write and in what styles, languages, alphabets and so on is a problem that can wait. Although I must say that I feel truly done in by Sonia's speech on the virtues of peace. No, I mean it,' he said hastily as Sonia started to bristle. 'I can't help talking smart like this, and you know it from way back, so don't be so prickly. But first things first, and first is this: How in the name of the Great Pumpkin do we get at an intercontinental jet plane long enough to write diddly-squat on it, without being carted away?'

'We'll have to do some research,' Dorc said.

'But what kind of research, man? You don't find answers to this kind of question in the public library.'

'You might,' Dorc said stubbornly. 'You might find out what the procedures are when they're getting a plane ready to go.'

'Why not go to the airport?' I said, and immediately wished I hadn't. They all looked at me with gleams of speculation in their eyes.

'Hey, Steve,' Dorc said in a far too admiring voice. 'That's a truly stellar thought, and I think I know just the man for the job.'

'Not me,' I said. 'Look at me. I'd be arrested the minute I asked some airport person what time it was.'

'I am looking at you,' Dorc answered, 'and what I see beneath the buttons and the tatters is a perfect little gentleman. I see a bright and eager preppie who can always talk to the grown-ups in their own language and whose interest in the operations of a major airport could simply not be more natural. They may even take you for an airline heir.'

'Dorc, you rat-fink! I will not dress up like a preppie and go weaseling around the airport asking questions. Forget it!' I was genuinely furious, and also alarmed, since I knew he was right. They were all smart and good-looking in their own ways, but I was the only true-blue WASP of the lot.

'You have the clothes,' Dorc continued inexorably. 'Gray flannel pants, loafers, several Brooks Brothers shirts, even an excellent, sober tie, but that would be going too far.'

'No,' I said. 'No, no, no and again NO!'

'Think of it as an acting part,' Will said. 'Think of it as a great role which, even against your will, you have prepared to perfection.'

'I won't do it, and I certainly won't do it alone,' I added unwisely.

This, of course, was the breach in the wall, and to my

total astonishment, Sonia jumped into it. 'I'll go,' she said. 'I'll get all tarted up, and what Steve can't find out with his methods, maybe I can find out with mine.' She gave, as far as the booth permitted, a lascivious wiggle, and we all laughed. I could see I was hooked, but somehow it didn't seem so bad now that Sonia was going to join the charade. Of course, she would be playing a part she sometimes enjoyed, while I had one I hated and would only play on rare occasions, to please my family. Still, it might not be so bad. At least I wouldn't meet anyone I knew. My classmates were not big international travelers.

'Well, it's great to have one thing settled,' Dorc said, as if our poking around at the airport would automatically solve all the problems connected with this mad project.

Sonia consulted some sort of inner calendar. 'Let's go Friday,' she said. 'We can take the Train to the Plane.'

'Eight dollars out of my allowance,' I said gloomily. My allowance was generous by most kids' standards, but it never lasted the week. Having fun in New York was an expensive business, and this meant giving up almost two movies.

'Grin and bear it for once,' Will said. 'I think we're going to need a war chest for this project, and when we have something in it, maybe you'll get reimbursed. I'll see what I can squeeze out of the judge.'

'Money from the judge for graffiti,' Sonia gasped. 'Man, you've got to be right straight out of your mind, but please try, Will. It's no joke for me either to lay out that kind of money, and we're going to have a lot of expenses. This trip is only the start, you know.'

'Or only the finish,' Dorc said cynically. 'What you'll probably find out is that there is just no way it can be done, and we'll have to go back to deciding which handball court to immortalize.'

'I won't believe that!' Sonia was ready for battle again, but I got up and put on my coat. I was beginning to tire of all this excitement, and I wanted to be alone for a while.

'Got to go,' I said. 'Cosmic mountains of homework, don't you know. Think about what time we should go, Sonia, and I'll meet you, if I can find something to throw over my costume on the way to the train. What my mother would think if she saw me dressed like that is hard to imagine.'

'She'd send for the men in the white coats,' Sonia said. ''Bye, darlin'. I'm looking forward to our date.'

With a rude gesture to Sonia and a grim nod to the other two, I ambled out of the pits.

CHAPTER 5

The suspicion that I was soon going to feel terrible grew as I plodded toward the subway. The sky had clouded over again, and my portfolio felt as if it were full of bricks. High school art students carry their books as well as pictures and art supplies in their portfolios, so this is no exaggeration. I thought about the escalator being broken in my home station, and this added to my sense of grievance. Disgusting subways deserved to be bombed by the toys with their dimwitted scribblings. The great pieces which regularly appeared on the sides of the trains, only to be buffed into muddy, unrecognizable horrors, were too good for the New York subway system.

In another mood I would have admitted that for all its hideous faults, I had a sneaking fondness for the subway. I think all New York kids do, except for the few who are so rich they go everywhere in cabs and chauffered cars. Besides taking us to and from school (a dubious blessing), the battered old trains took us to our friends, to rock clubs, movies, museums or just to hang out someplace different. As magic carpets they were pretty moth-eaten, but they served the same purpose: they carried us out of the humdrum world and towards what we always hoped would be something better. Almost everyone became an expert at getting from A to B on one token (my lapses were mostly the result of inattention), and we felt at home in our ugly, rattling carriages.

This afternoon, however, hostility was gaining the upper hand. As I went down the stairs, I checked out a few inexpert tags that had appeared overnight and thought of 'Griffin Man'. He hadn't called me, but then, why would he? It was rush hour, and, as usual, no one bothered to check my pass. Just let it get one day out of date though, and they'd be all over me like flies. The train, when it came, was the usual sardine can. I wedged myself in, trying to put my portfolio someplace that would be sub-lethal. After a bit a huge black man came over and stood on my foot. I know this sounds paranoid, and it may have been an accident, but if it was, why didn't he get off? 'Yo, man,' I said, trying to sound amiable. 'That's my foot you're standing on.'

'Then get your goddam foot outa my way, white boy,' he said.

This was a standard response, which didn't bother me as far as its wording went. It was the hatred behind the conventional phrase that got me down. It always did. I jerked my offending foot out from under his 250 pounds and lapsed into sullen silence. Why me? What had I done? I hadn't sold his wretched grandmother on the auction block or even made him ride on the back of any buses. Hell no. On the contrary here he was standing on my foot as if he owned it, and giving me shit besides. I had been brought up to understand this kind of anger, but nothing was going to make me like it. In school I was in the minority, and sometimes, as towering denizens of the ghetto swept past me on the escalators, or glared down at me in the cafeteria line, I wished I were black. When I got home again, to Brooklyn Heights, I would feel ashamed, knowing how lucky I was and how little I had had to do with it. A lot of things in life were going to be easier for me than for the black kids who so briefly lorded it over me in school.

My thoughts turned inevitably to Will. Did he hate me too, somewhere deep down inside? On the whole I thought not, or not any more than anyone else. Everybody hates everybody else a little for one stupid reason or another. Will had a lot of advantages, of course, but he also had a really sweet nature. Well, that was probably because of his advantages. But not necessarily. I'd known poor black people who were just as good natured, as well as a lot of mean sons of bitches. My thoughts went round and round as the train alternately rocketed and crawled towards home. One thing was sure; this incident had given me the final, downward push. Now, if something marvelous had happened on the subway (and this was not unheard of), it might have reversed the whole ghastly trend.

As it was, by the time I had climbed up out of the depths of the High Street station and then climbed the three flights of stairs to our apartment, I had all my guns loaded for my poor mother. (Sure it's healthy to live in a fourth floor walk-up, but not when you come home to one of the deepest subway stations in New York and the escalator is broken and you're carrying two tons of books. Besides, the school is six storeys, and the escalators there are always broken. This is why I don't give vigorous-looking old ladies my subway seat on the rare occasions that I have a seat to give. They can stand there and glare their little old hearts out. I'm a lot more pooped than they are.)

Anyway, I stamped through the front door ready for something to be wrong, and of course, at such times something always is. I opened the refrigerator door with a feeling of foreboding, and sure enough there was nothing to drink – no juice, no milk, no soda, nothing.

'There's nothing to drink,' I howled.

My mother was standing at the stove stirring one of those complicated messes which sometimes seem to be the sole object of my parents' marriage. Too busy to think of any beverage but wine which she, by the way, was drinking. 'Have a glass of wine,' she said amiably. 'I'm going to the store in a few minutes.'

'I hate wine.'

'Why, Steve,' she said. 'This is something new.'

She should have known where the conversation would go from this point, but she wasn't thinking. Anyway there isn't much she can do right when I get this way. The scene pretty much has to play itself out. 'I hate *this* wine,' I declared. 'Why can't we ever have any decent wine?'

'This is perfectly good wine for everyday,' she answered somewhat huffily. 'You can't expect some great vintage every day.'

'Not a great vintage, just something that doesn't taste like sheep piss. I suppose we're broke,' I added, which not only served to fuel the fire, but also expressed one of my deepest fears.

'Not broke, just at the careful stage,' my mother said soothingly.

This was worse than I had expected. After all, we always drink jug wine except when we have company. It's not necessarily anything to get alarmed about. 'I know what that means,' I groaned. 'From careful to broke is just one baby step.'

'Now Steve, you know that's not true – not always true,' she amended with her usual fairness. 'We should have a big check any day now.'

My parents' fortunes went up and down like Yo-Yos, and their persistent optimism during the down periods was enough to drive anyone up the wall. 'Any day. Any day. Any month, you mean. Any year. Don't give me that bull, please. Just don't. I don't want to hear it.' I was working myself into a real funk now – getting really upset instead of just depressed and irritable, and I couldn't reverse the process.

My mother could see it building, too, and it was a toss-up whether she would sit down and listen to me for an hour or opt out and let the wave ebb by itself. This time she had a good excuse. She turned the flame down low under the mess and said firmly, 'Steve, I really can't go through it tonight. I'll go get you something to drink, and then you can have a snack, and maybe you'll feel better.'

So she marched off to the supermarket, and I went into my room and threw myself down in front of the tube. The steady procession of idiots across the screen was soothing. Almost imperceptibly, my spirits began to rise. I even chuckled once or twice at some inane jokes. By the time my mother had come home and I'd had some milk and munchies, I was good old jolly Steve again. Just call me Dr Jekyll and Mr Hyde. Fortunately these moods don't come so often anymore, and sometimes I can even kill them off before they get a good start. My mother isn't always so saintly either. If she hadn't gone to the store this time, she might have ended up yelling right back, even though she knows this is the worst thing to do. Leaving me to my own devices is probably the best idea. It doesn't call for reserves of patience she may not have.

While gathering strength to crunch into my homework, I went out to the kitchen again. I could see that my mother was relieved that the storm was over and glad to have my company as she chopped, stirred and simmered. We chatted about this and that, and at one point she put down her spoon and ran off to get a *New Yorker* cartoon she knew I would like. It was a comfortable scene. I didn't even mind when she asked with elaborate casualness how much homework I had. My parents were deliberately, sometimes even painfully, cool about homework. You could see that the temptation to nag was sometimes almost overwhelming, but nag they would not. My school career was my business, and if I wanted to foul it up, that was my business too. I was supposed to be smart enough to see that I wouldn't get anywhere without gluing the seat of my pants to the old desk chair once in a while. This was actually pretty heavy, like a lot of the other responsibilities they laid on me, but it was beginning to work out the way they thought it would. More and more was getting done, and my grades, with the exception of math, in which I maintained a steady D, were fairly marvelous. Of course, they could have been better, but a nightly battle about homework would certainly have brought them down. The two old foxes were clever enough to know that. Sometimes I envied kids whose parents told them every breath to draw, but each time I thought about changing places with one of them and taking all that flak, I decided it was better to stagger along trying to be adult before my time.

Just as I was leaving the kitchen, my mother said, 'Hey, have you done anything for the art show yet? It's only a week away, you know.' (This was an area in which she felt a good push would not be taken amiss.)

I came back, more than ready to waste a little more time on a favorite subject. 'Mum, I can do it in one night,' I said. 'You know that.'

'I know you can, but why? Wouldn't it be better if you gave it more time?'

'Not necessarily,' I said. 'I'm still thinking about what to do. What would you say to a graffiti piece?'

She gave this more thought than I would have expected. 'Not much,' she said finally. 'They don't belong in frames.'

'Not in a frame. A frame would look stupid. Just a huge piece of paper, maybe frayed at the edges.'

'No,' she said. 'They belong out of doors or on trains. That's what the style is all about.'

'Mother! You astonish me,' I said in tones of genteel horror.

'Don't get me wrong,' she said. 'I hate all that stuff inside the subway cars. It's ugly and senseless and has about as much in common with art as a bunch of animal tracks – less, in fact. Animal tracks can be beautiful.'

'It's not all bad,' I protested. 'If you study it, you can see who's been there.'

'Well, maybe you can read it like some sort of underground newspaper,' she said, 'but I can't and, furthermore, I don't want to. To me it just looks like hell, and that's that. But the outsides of the trains are another matter. When I'm standing there, bored to death with all that gringy gray around me, and a car comes flashing by with big, bright letters on it, everything suddenly seems much cheerier. It makes me sick to see all those lovely colors ruined by the buffers.'

This revealed a side of my mother which I might have guessed at, but hadn't. 'So you approve of subway graffiti?' I asked cautiously.

'Outside, not inside,' she answered. 'Why can't the MTA give them the outsides of the cars and spend their money cleaning and policing the insides?'

'That's stupid,' I said. 'It wouldn't work. You know half the point of doing graffiti is that they're illegal. The taggers aren't going to leave the insides of the cars alone just because they can do the outsides legally. In the first place, you're taking half the fun out of it. In the second place, you're talking about two completely different kinds of graffiti. A big piece takes hours. It's done by a crew in the yards or on a siding, and the good ones are all planned out ahead of time. A tag is done very quickly, on the sly, usually with just a single-color marker. It's just a way of leaving your name in as many places as possible, which is all a lot of people care about. I guess you could say that a big piece is the tag to end all tags; but not everyone wants to plan that much or take that much risk or work with a crew. So the two things are connected but different.'

'I still wish we could dispense with all that scribbling,' she said stubbornly.

'Listen,' I said. 'The good graffiti artists are against defacement. They don't write on windows or maps or monuments. That kind of thing is done by juveniles – we call them "toys" – kids who just want to get in on the scene and mess things up as much as they can.'

My mother is no slouch. She caught that single 'we' on the fly and sent it right back across the net. 'I suppose you're into this graffiti scene, too,' she said.

'I do the stray tag here and there,' I admitted. 'All of excellent quality and taste, of course.'

'Of course. That goes without saying. What happens if you get caught?'

'A fine, I guess, for a first offence, just tagging. But I won't get caught. Don't worry. I only do it when there's nobody for miles around.'

'You wouldn't, of course, dream of doing a piece?' she said, in the tones of one who knows better but still hopes for the best.

'Well, I might *dream* of it,' I said carefully, 'but you

wouldn't catch me dead in the train yards, or probably dead is how you would catch me if I went there. So don't worry about that. Besides I'm not getting carted off to any so-called juvenile facility. I'd be broken down into my component parts – a finger here, an eyeball there – inside half an hour.'

'A sobering thought,' she said, trying to keep it light, and then with heavy emphasis, '*Do be careful*, Steve. Even a fine at this point would definitely not be welcome. Right?'

'Right, Mum,' I said cheerfully. 'Don't worry. I know what I'm doing.'

I started to fade out of the kitchen again, and she half turned back to her pots muttering something about devoutly hoping so. Then another thought struck her: 'Oh, Steve,' she called. 'I forgot to tell you, and I don't know what made me think of it now. I got a weird phone call.' I was back in the kitchen in a flash. 'Someone wanting the Troll King. Would that be you, by any chance?'

'Who else? When did he call?'

'About five. He said he'd call back.'

'Try to get a number if I'm not here,' I begged. 'This is a dude I really want to talk to.'

'I'll try,' she said dubiously. 'He didn't sound very forthcoming.'

'No, he wouldn't probably,' I said. I had the sudden feeling that I could glimpse the shy, mysterious personality of Griffin Man behind this trivial exchange. 'Just try. OK?'

'All right, I'll try.' She turned firmly back to her cooking this time, and I galloped off to my room feeling oddly cheered by the thought that something had actually come of my message in the Canal Street station.

I did my homework, adorning it heavily with bits of artistic genius. The medieval manuscript copiers had nothing on me, except that their capitals and margins were of a more uplifting nature. Teachers in art high schools put up with this sort of thing, and some even regard it as a bonus. This is just as well, since most of us do it almost instinctively, and it enlivens many an otherwise dreary assignment. They even let us draw in class, so long as the eyes we occasionally raise have some spark of life in them. I, for one, can draw, answer homework questions, and watch the tube all at the same time. In this way, the time passed peacefully until our usual late dinner hour.

CHAPTER 6

Except for the rare weekend day when all my friends are busy and I languish at home, my life tends to be more exciting than anyone would really want. Nothing, however, happened between the Tuesday gathering at the pits and Friday, the day Sonia and I had agreed on for our trip to the airport. The total absence of people trying to mug me, teachers threatening to crucify me and other colorful incidents made me even more nervous about the projected trip. Griffin Man didn't call. Sonia did call to fix a time for our departure. I said hopefully that my parents were low on funds and I probably couldn't raise the fare, but she said Will had acquired some money somehow and she'd get it from him. Since there was no obvious way out, I agreed to meet her at Broadway-Nassau at seven o'clock Friday night.

The gray flannel pants still fit if I wore them down on my hips a bit. (Cheer up, boy. There's been a little growth since the last formal occasion.) I also wore a pale blue shetland sweater over a cream colored Brooks Brothers shirt open at the neck and brown loafers only slightly pinching in the toe. My hair shone with cleanliness and brushing, but then, it always did. A glance in the mirror stirred the deep-down, nasty suspicion that I really looked pretty good. If I ever decided to change my persona, my father would cheerfully lay the family fortunes at the door of BB, but that would be far in the future, if ever. I really didn't have the chutzpah to carry off this style at school as if it were just another costume. Besides, I liked looking disreputable. It was amusing and comfortable, and with my deceptively studious face, it kept everyone guessing. I threw my black opera cloak over the ensemble and headed for the door. Our apartment, however, is too small to get out of unseen. My mother looked up from a book and said, 'Going to a fancy-dress ball, dear?'

'Just more cosmic funkiness,' I said evasively, all the while keeping the couch between us so she couldn't see my elegant feet. 'I'll see you whenever, dear old Mum.'

'Where are you going, just for curiosity?' she asked.

Normally I don't mind a little mild curiosity, but not tonight, of all times. 'Meeting Sonia,' I mumbled with more truth than wisdom.

'*That* luscious wench!' my mother said.

'Go find a time warp and jump through it,' I answered. 'She's nothing of the sort, at least not to me. And now, GOODBYE.' And I oozed rapidly out the door before she could have any more bright conversational ideas.

Broadway-Nassau is one of the stops for the Train to the Plane and also the junction of many subway lines. Sonia was waiting for me on the platform, and I had to swallow a couple of times and put my mother's funny remarks out of my mind when I saw her. She was wearing heels and a form-fitting, bright orange dress, which sounds pretty vulgar but wasn't. Her figure is willowy, but she is by no means flat-chested; and the dress, which was some very nice, soft material, looked as if it had been made for or maybe on her. She also looked about seven feet tall. The thick, shiny black braid hanging down to her waist added to this effect and gave her an innocent-but-sexy look which was just right for this occasion (or any other for that matter).

'Yo! Sonia!' I called.

She turned and looked at me and laughed. 'Oh, Steve, you look like a pocket phantom of the opera. Take that thing off and let me see how gorgeous you are.'

I glared at her and then glanced around the station. 'Somebody might think I just came in from boarding-school,' I protested.

'Nobody down here cares if you just came in from Mars,' she said. 'Take it off. You must be roasting.'

She had a point there, so I eased out of the cloak and immediately felt much cooler, if a trifle naked. 'Satisfied?' I asked, draping the heavy thing stylishly over my arm.

'But you look fantastic, Steve,' she said with a sincerity that embarrassed me almost to extinction. 'You know, we shouldn't stop with just going to the airport. We should get on a plane and fly away to Europe, go to some grand hotel and dance until dawn.'

I had visions of myself dancing with Sonia, my nose fondly nuzzling her navel – well, maybe her collar bone. She had elegant collar bones, well displayed by the scoop of her dress. What I said was, 'Yeah. Compared with painting a plane, stowing away on one ought to be child's play.'

'Don't be so practical,' Sonia said. 'Do you like my dress?' The inevitable question.

'You should be hard to lose in a crowd,' I said heartlessly, but she looked genuinely crushed, so I had to say, 'No, really, Sonia, it's terrific. You absolutely look like Wow, and I mean it.' And since I did, she was immediately her old bouncy self again.

At this point the Train to the Plane slid into the station, so we got on board and settled into seats which were just subway seats, but the nice kind and incredibly clean. Everything, in fact, was very spruce, and I thought of my mother saying that if just the insides of subways were clean it would be enough to make her happy. I had to admit that even if this was only a glorified subway car, it had an atmosphere of peacefulness and safety and even a certain luxuriousness about it. All that from a little cleanliness. I wouldn't have believed it.

Sonia handed me a ten. 'Pay for us both,' she said. 'It'll look respectable.'

'Who cares?' I asked, marveling at this new, middle-class Sonia.

'We have to practice – get in the mood. At least you do.'

'Oh great,' I said. 'Don't remind me, please.'

'You're going to be a smash hit. Why are you always so pessimistic?'

'Who, me? You've got me mixed up with Dorc. If I didn't have an idiotically bright outlook on life, we wouldn't be here.'

'It seems to me,' Sonia said, 'that ever since you had the idea about the plane, you've been trying to talk everybody out of it.'

'Well, since it was my idea, I wanted to be on record for having had some sense when the whole thing came crashing down about our ears.'

'You see what I mean?' she said. 'Just stop making all those ominous remarks. Everything is going to be perfect.'

I gave her one of my most cynical looks, and we both lapsed into silence. The Train to the Plane runs on one of the less ravaged subway tracks, and the cars are pretty new, so conversation is possible at some level below a shriek. But silence is even easier.

After a while Sonia reached into her enormous bag and brought out a pad and pen. I cursed myself for coming away without one. This must have been the result of my drastic clothes change, since I was usually equipped to draw in any circumstances. For the moment I had to content myself with looking over her shoulder. Sonia was drawing flowers, a nice feminine occupation, you could say, except that these were the kind of flowers you might meet on a not very friendly planet somewhere in the Crab Nebula. They were beautiful in a distinctly ferocious way, and I thought of her color pictures I had seen in school. Sonia used color in a way that made shivers go up and down my spine. Besides flowers, she also specialized in clouds, fires, explosions, anything in which colors moved and shifted into each other. Some of her images were violent, but most were just wonderfully rich and sensuous.

Sonia apparently sensed my envious gaze and itching fingers because she looked up and said, 'Oh, poor baby. Nothing to do with your hands?' and delved into her bag again, coming up with another small pad and a very acceptable pen. From that point the dull trip passed quickly. Like most New York art students, we were both able to draw fairly well on the subway. Whatever unexpected squiggles resulted from the sway and stagger of the train were simply incorporated into the design. It was a challenge.

After a while, the train came up out of the ground, and we were able to look out over that strange world which is the outer edge of Brooklyn. I say 'strange', and I mean it, although I suppose there is nothing more banal than these flat miles of little houses all so much alike, marching on and on, punctuated here and there by vacant lots or clusters of depressing-looking stores. To people who spend their lives in Manhattan or Brooklyn Heights, this is like another planet. It was getting dark, and the street lights had come on, which somehow made the long streets look even more forlorn. I tried to imagine real kids like me and Sonia growing up here, meeting friends, maybe in that disconsolate-looking pizza shack that we were passing, having bright ideas and making witty remarks to each other. I even knew people at school who came in from places like this, but still my imagination failed me. Probably I'm some terrible kind of snob, but you can't imagine something you've never experienced.

Our super-subway was stopping now at a place called Howard Beach. Sonia and I looked at each other dubiously. 'I think this is it,' I said. 'Never heard of it, but it seems to be the end of the line.'

'Well, here goes, Steve,' Sonia said, and stuffed her drawing things back into her bag. I hung onto mine on the theory that at an airport you never could tell when you might have to kill some time.

We came off the platform into a surprisingly pleasant little station. At the end of a ramp the bus to the airport was waiting. The driver was holding out his hand, so I put my train ticket in it, hoping that this was the right thing to do. 'Where to?' he asked crisply.

I wasn't ready for this, but I made a lightning decision. 'London,' I said.

To my horror, the man laughed. 'What airline, son?'

'Oh, excuse me. Pan Am,' I said, with what I hoped was the proper degree of casualness.

'Pan Am departures,' he said, and waved us to the interior of the bus.

CHAPTER 7

The scene which greeted us when we entered the Pan Am departures lounge was familiar to me, if not to Sonia. It was perhaps the busiest time of night for European departures, and I felt a stir of excitement that had nothing to do with our mission as we watched the bustling, purposeful activity around the ticket counters. Sonia apparently felt it too, because she squeezed my arm and said, 'Oh, Steve, I wish we were going someplace too.'

'I know what you mean,' I said. 'Actually there's nothing duller than long air trips, but there's something about the idea of getting on a plane and taking off for somewhere that gets to you.'

'I went to Puerto Rico when I was little,' Sonia said, 'but I don't remember much about the trip. Besides this seems more important. These people are going to Europe.'

I tried to look jaded and world-weary. 'It's all the same,' I said. 'Europe, Puerto Rico, California, Japan. The question is, what are we going to do now?'

'I thought you would know.'

'I think we're too early,' I said. 'Everybody is busy, and this would definitely not be the time of night to even think of pulling anything. Maybe if we wander over to one of the departure gates, we'll find someone to talk to. Now look, we'll probably end up talking to different people in different places, so let's decide where to meet. There's a coffee shop over there with a view of the field. When you think you've done all you can, go there and look for me or I'll look for you. OK?'

'OK? What do you mean, OK? I don't have a clue, Steve.' Sonia was looking around desperately, and it was clearly all very different from what she had imagined.

'Find some nice, sexy-looking dude in a uniform and make lively conversation,' I said unsympathetically, and started to move off towards gate nine, where I had spied a clean-cut type in a white shirt with something written on the pocket. He wasn't doing anything at the moment, and I felt an urge to tackle the problem swiftly, head on, before I lost my nerve. I glanced back at Sonia, who stood alone, looking forlorn but beautiful in her orange dress. 'She's going to be picked up by somebody who doesn't know an airplane from his ass,' I muttered, but to my relief, she made a horrible face and a rude gesture at me and swung away, swishing her hips. She would probably find the right victim without any help from me.

Meanwhile, I was closing in on my target. On closer inspection he looked even more wholesome and helpful, and I could see what it said on his shirt pocket, 'Ed Germaine'. This was not really informative, but it was not discouraging either. 'Hi, er, Mr Germaine,' I said in a firm, bright voice.

'Hi, there. How are you?'

'Oh, I'm fine, thank you,' I said. 'Nice night for flying.'

'Just fine, just fine,' said Mr Germaine, and I wondered desperately what inanity I could think up next. Apparently, however, I had turned him on a little, because he spoke again. 'You flying out tonight?'

'No, I just saw my parents off for London,' I said, hoping again that this was a good choice. There were always lots of planes for London.

'Ah. Too bad you couldn't go. Great place, London.'

'Oh, I know,' I said, 'but I've been there so many times. Actually I could have gone, but I have a lot to do in the city just now, so I thought I'd give this one the miss.'

'Big traveler, are you?' he asked.

'Every spring London, every fall Rome, and then, of course, various places in the summer.' I hoped I wasn't overdoing it, but he nodded sagely. International kids were an old story to him, I was glad to see.

'Well,' he said, 'it probably gets to be a drag, in and out of airports all the time.'

I could see by now that this conversation wasn't going anywhere without a big push, and he had given me just a tiny crack to put a crowbar in. I took a deep breath and plunged. 'The thing is, Mr Germaine, when you're getting on a plane to go somewhere, you never really see very much, and I've gotten interested in, you know, what really goes on at an airport. But all I ever see is the ticket counter and the boarding gate, and then you go down a long tube and you're on the plane. I'd like to see what goes on out on the field when they're getting the planes ready to take off. Is there some sort of tour a person could take?'

'Onto the field?' he asked, looking scandalized.

'Well, yes, or to the hangars or, you know, just around outside the passenger terminals . . .'

Mr Germaine seemed to be inflating himself, getting ready for some weighty pronouncement. 'Son,' he said. 'Nobody goes on that field without a pass and that includes me and all the airline officials.'

'What about the people who take things to the planes, food and that sort of thing?'

'The caterers? They all have passes, believe you me – passes with their pictures, and they're checked very carefully.'

'Well, I can see how that would be necessary,' I said, 'what with all the bomb scares and hijacking and whatnot. You couldn't let just anybody wander around out there. Why some of those kids might get in and start painting graffiti on the planes the way they do on the subway cars.' This transition seemed weak to me, but I tried to make it sound like a small, maybe not very funny, joke.

To my alarm, Mr Germaine swelled even more and turned quite red in the face. I had apparently hit him on a sensitive spot, but it soon became clear that his wrath was not directed at me. 'Those punks had better not try anything out here,' he snarled. 'We know how to deal with that sort of thing.'

'You do?'

'You bet your sweet life we do. This place isn't run by the MTA you know.'

'I know.'

'There's money out here, and don't you forget it. Big money.'

'Yes, sir. I'm sure there must be.'

' 'Course, if they'd let Mayor Koch have his way in the city, maybe they could take care of those goons. Mayor Koch wants to put wolves in the train yards,' he finished triumphantly.

'Wolves?' I said. I was feeling badly shaken up.

'Wolves!' he cried. 'Not dogs, wolves.'

'Oh hey,' I said in a small voice. 'I mean, that is a really hairy idea.' It was beginning to occur to me that the mayor had been indulging in one of his famous little jokes at the expense of God knows who, but now was not the time for a giggle. Also, I seemed to have led the conversation far afield. I hadn't found out anything useful, and it didn't look as if there were anything useful to find out. All that remained was to get away from this maniac as gracefully as possible.

'You bet it is,' Mr Germaine said, referring with relish to the idea of all those poor graffiti artists being rended by slavering beasts. 'But anyway, that isn't a problem at the airport. We have more serious problems here, but I like to think that we have one of the tightest security systems in the world. Our guards are smart fellas. They're not going to let anybody get out there who isn't fully authorized.'

'I guess what I was really asking,' I said humbly, 'is whether there wasn't some way for a curious person like me – someone who was really just interested in airports – to see a little more of what goes on. But the answer seems to be no.'

Mr Germaine deflated a bit and looked at me kindly. 'Why don't you go up to the parking level on the fourth floor?' he said. 'There's an observation walk all around, and you can see about as much from there as you could from anywhere. Take the elevator right over there, and get off on four.'

'OK. I'll do that,' I said brightly. 'Thanks a lot, Mr Germaine. It was really interesting talking to you.'

'That's OK, son. Come on back and chat some more if you want to.'

I smiled a grateful, respectful smile and made off for the elevator he had pointed out. What a disaster. At least I could go up on the roof and recover my wits, but I doubted that I would learn much.

The parking area turned out to be a rather spooky

space. It was very dark, and there was surprisingly little activity, considering that this was a busy time for the airport. I went over to the edge and stood looking out into the night. I could see gigantic tail fins maneuvering in the distance, lights of various colors, low buildings which presumably served some maintenance function scattered here and there. Moving around a corner, I found that from this spot I could at least see a whole plane. It was some distance away, however, and while I could see a couple of small trucks drawn up close to it, I couldn't tell what they were doing. On the whole, the scene was bleak and daunting. It was foreign, forbidden territory, and it seemed to me that far more than a pass stood between me and the great shining flanks of the plane. Out there I would be like Frodo in Mordor – a tiny figure wandering in a great darkness where there were no familiar signposts. The wind that came off the field had turned cold and was starting to creep into my shetland sweater, so I decided to give up on my researches and go back to the lounge. Maybe, by some miracle, my partner had had better luck.

CHAPTER 8

I skirted the area around gate nine cautiously, but Mr Germaine was not in sight. In the coffee shop I spotted Sonia immediately, sitting at a table near the window. She was drooping over a cup of coffee, and I could tell right away that her methods had yielded no better news than mine. I had never seen Sonia really discouraged before, and it was a demoralizing sight. The flame-colored dress was slightly askew over the beautiful collar bones, and even her shiny braid looked frazzled at the edges. I slid into the seat across from her and made a gruesome face.

'You can say that again,' Sonia said. 'What a washout. What a complete, total, disgusting waste of time, money and good clothes.'

'What happened?' I asked. 'You found somebody, didn't you?'

'Oh I found somebody. I found the original friendly ape, a sort of guard type, and he would cheerfully have talked to me all night for the privilege of gazing down my front as he gabbled.'

'He must have been tall,' I said enviously.

'He was tall enough,' Sonia said sharply, 'and dumb

enough, but I'm afraid he knew what he was talking about.'

'Why? What did he say?'

'He said, "No way," ' Sonia answered, and in spite of herself, she gave the ghost of a giggle. 'And he kept saying it. "No way, baby. There is no way. There is just no way you can go out on that field. I mean there is no way." On and on like that, shaking his head back and forth. It was hypnotic. He finally got me doing it too. So we just stood there saying the same stupid words. I would say, "So there's really no way?" and he would answer, "No way".' Sonia's sense of comedy was coming to her rescue, at least temporarily. 'So finally he asked me to come to the bar and have a drink, and I said . . .' She paused for effect.

'No way!' I supplied.

Sonia laughed and nodded her head, but then she remembered what all of this meant to us, and she drooped again. 'Steve, it's terrible. You have to have a very special pass with your picture on it to get out on the field at any time of day, and even if I could find some guy who liked me well enough to break all the rules and take me out there with him, what good would that do the rest of us? Even if I just wanted to do something by myself, which I don't, I wouldn't have a chance with some hairy boob trotting along showing me all the sights. What about your important WASPish official? By the look on your face you either didn't find one or wish you hadn't.'

'I found one all right. He wasn't that important, but he knew everything down to the last depressing detail.' I told her about my encounter with Mr Germaine and its discouraging result.

Sonia looked thoughtful. 'You know,' she said, 'I did find out one thing and that's the fact that late at night things get pretty thin around here. If we could get passes somehow and pretend we were taking food or toilet paper or something out to a plane that was being serviced at around three a.m., maybe we could get away with it.'

'Yeah, for about ten minutes at the most,' I said. 'Mr Germaine says they have the tightest security system in the world here.'

'I don't like the sound of that,' Sonia said.

'I don't like the whole repulsive situation,' I answered, and we lapsed into gloomy silence. I even forgot that I still had an extra dollar of Will's money that could have been spent on something reviving. My appetite had gone the way of my hopes, down the drain. We both stared out the window at the big, silvery plane that was standing there and ground our teeth in frustration. All that lovely, clean empty surface just waiting for us and no way to get at it. 'I could go jump in the Sound, Gucci loafers and all,' I mumbled.

Sonia's eyes brightened with a brief, mad gleam. 'Steve. That's an idea!'

'It is, but I think I won't, if you don't mind. Life still holds out some promise in other areas after all, and poor Mummy and Daddy just would not understand.'

'Not jumping in the Sound, idiot,' Sonia snapped. 'I mean maybe we could come in by boat and sort of creep up on some plane in the dead of night.'

'We'd still get caught before we could do anything, and besides, who's got a boat? For Christ's sake, Sonia. What a dumb idea.' I hadn't meant to sound so mean, but that's the way I felt.

Sonia was never one to take an insult lying down. 'All right, so think of a better one, super brain,' she shot back. 'You were the one who gave the fine speech about doing the impossible and how we should rap about all the wild and wooly ways things could be done.'

'It's different in Dorc's room,' I said, 'or at the pits or somewhere like that. This place gives me a chill.'

'You still don't have to put me down every time I open my mouth,' Sonia complained.

'Sonia, I'm not putting you down,' I said as patiently as I could. 'I'm sorry, I just feel rotten. OK?'

'Yeah, me too,' she said, subsiding into gloom. 'So what are we going to do?'

'Go home and tell Will and Dorc that it's all off,' I said. 'What else can we do? We'll just have to think of something else.'

Sonia kicked the table with one delicately shod foot, and the pain made her even angrier. 'I don't want to think of something else. This is the only thing I want to think of, and if you're going to get together and talk about what stupid wall you're going to paint, you can do it without me. You three guys are just too middle class to live.'

Under the circumstances this was something of a *non sequitur*, but it seemed unwise to point it out. Instead I said, 'Come on, Sonia. It wouldn't be the same without you.'

'Oh, you make me tired, you three. I'm going to form a crew of girls, and then you'll see. You and Carlos too.'

'Where are you going to find them?' I said nastily. There had been great female graffiti artists, and there certainly would be again, but it wasn't common; and at the moment, so far as I knew, Sonia was the only one who even had the potential for doing a big piece. Naturally, this was not the most tactful thing to say, but I didn't care. What I could live without just now was a big dose of feminist propaganda. Of course, that's just what I got.

'There are lots of girls who are as good as you are, smart ass. They just don't go around shooting their mouths off about how marvelous they are and how they're going to do this or that fantastic piece. That doesn't mean they don't exist.'

This, at least in respect to my retiring, un-macho image, was so unfair it took my breath away. 'Name one,' I snarled.

Sonia gave me a glare of truly terrifying Hispanic venom. 'Why should I?' she said furiously, and then, for no reason I could see, she sat back in her chair and laughed. 'Oh, Steve, look at us. All dressed up like some married couple off to Europe and already at each other's throats. What will we be like by the time we reach the city of our dreams?'

'You'll be nasty in Naples and vile in Vienna,' I suggested.

'There'll be bruises in Brussels and punches in Paris.'

'What's beastly in Berlin will turn rotten in Rotterdam.'

'And be hell in Helsinki.'

'We'll growl in Grenoble and divorce in Dubrovnik,' I cried, dredging the bottom of my geographical barrel.

'And do murder in Munich,' Sonia finished triumphantly.

We sat back and beamed at each other, overcome by our own cleverness. 'You know what would be fun, Steve?' Sonia said. 'We can't just get on that boring train and go home with our dismal news. Let's see if we can get a drink in that really cool-looking bar. I've still got some money tucked away for emergencies, and I think this is an emergency.'

'They'll never serve us,' I protested. Sonia was sixteen and looked older, especially today, but as for me, forget it. 'Kennedy airport is no rock club,' I added unnecessarily.

'No, but it's the other end of the scale,' Sonia replied. 'It's so respectable they won't even think about our age. Anyway, don't underestimate me. It's worth a try.'

In fact, between Sonia's imperious beauty and my incredibly clean-cut look, we brought it off and soon found ourselves elegantly ensconced in low chairs with a small table between us and a potted tree leaning over my shoulder. We were near the window and could see another splendid plane wheeling up, but for the moment, we had decided to put this tantalizing sight out of our minds and concentrate on our minor adventure.

'What shall we have?' I asked in a low voice, not wanting to fumble the ball when the waiter arrived.

Sonia appeared to be studying something in her lap. I deduced that she was counting her worldly wealth before reaching a decision. 'Something with a lot of alcohol for the money,' she said. 'Maybe dry martinis?'

'I've never had one,' I confessed. 'Aren't they rather repellent?'

'Not that bad,' Sonia said, 'and you get a lot of mileage out of one. Order doubles, and then we'll see where we are when we've paid for them.'

'Who me, order? You're out of your mind.'

'It's the only way,' Sonia assured me solemnly. 'You're the man, and besides, if you don't brazen it out, they'll be sure to ask for ID.'

The waiter, a tall, hollow-cheeked type who reminded me of the butler in a horror flick, was drifting our way. When he finally arrived, I gave him my most aristocratic stare. 'Two double martinis, please,' I said, 'and make them very dry, if you don't mind.'

'Up or on the rocks, sir?' he asked, never batting an eyelid. Maybe they were in the red at this bar and needed any customers they could get.

'Up,' I said, succinctly. It was no time to dither over minor details, and surely ice could only be a disadvantage. Sonia gave me an admiring look which was sufficient reward.

'Terrific,' she whispered when the waiter had sidled off. 'Absolutely cosmic, Steve. Here's a ten.' And she slipped me a bill under the table.

'Is this courtesy of Will, too?' I asked.

Sonia's eyes sparkled. 'This, my dear, is courtesy of Carlos, who would be even more horrified than the old judge if he knew what cause he was helping to support.'

The drinks came. They were pale and lethal looking but not, perhaps, very large. I eyed mine warily, but Sonia lifted her glass. 'Here's to them all,' she said. 'To the judge and Carlos and Mr Germaine and good brother "No Way"!'

'Confusion to the enemies of graffiti,' I added, and took a cautious swig. The taste certainly left something to be desired, but I could feel a very agreeable stirring in my veins after just one swallow. I took another and then one more.

'Make it last,' Sonia whispered, but she was laughing, and the couple of slugs she took were by no means minuscule.

After a minute though we did slow down. We were both beginning to feel just fine, and things which had seemed depressing a short while ago started to take on the rosy glow of possibility.

'Sonia,' I said, 'I've got a great idea. When all this is over – you know, when we've done the deed –' and I waved vaguely at the waiting plane, 'we'll do a beautiful mural for this bar as a token of our appreciation because it gave us the courage to carry on.'

'Fantastic,' Sonia said. 'I see just the place.'

We both eyed lovingly an expanse of bare wall at the end of the room and took reflective pulls at our martinis.

'We'll be famous by then, of course,' Sonia said dreamily. 'We can do a picture of the plane with our piece on it, and people will flock to this bar to see what it was like.'

'Yes, and then they won't have to serve obvious minors any more to keep from going broke.'

'Except for us, of course. Our drinks will be on the house.' Sonia was looking more and more her old self. In fact, she was looking a good deal better than her old self. I wondered briefly if this magical beverage was having the same effect on my appearance. Probably not, but I felt greatly improved, which amounted to much the same thing. A feeling of intimacy which I would never have believed possible was growing between us, and I was able to ignore some of the sterner facts of life such as the fact that Sonia was Dorc's girlfriend and that she was a year older and maybe eight inches taller than I was. I felt that it would be fine to sit here forever in this delicious atmosphere and talk about all kinds of things. There was a lot I had always wanted to know about Sonia and never had the nerve to ask. The subject of her famous brother was always a good opener, if normally a somewhat dangerous one.

'Sonia,' I said in my most mellow voice, 'we made one mistake when we proposed that toast.'

'Oh, did we? What?'

'Well, you can't call Carlos an enemy of graffiti. He's one of the biggest writers in the business. You can hardly take a train anywhere that you don't see one of his pieces, and those pieces really burn.'

'You don't have to tell me,' she said, 'but the point is, Steve, he's the enemy of *our* graffiti, so let's leave him right in there with the rest of the creeps.' She lifted her glass again, and I joined her. They were getting alarmingly low.

'What about your parents?' I said, even more daringly. 'What would they think? I mean, you do have parents?'

Sonia laughed. 'Of course I have parents, you twit. I even have two parents and they live together. In fact, they spend all their time together, which wouldn't be so hot if they had a minute to stop and think about it. They've got a *bodega* – you know – a mom-and-pop grocery store, and that's right where they are about fourteen hours a day, seven days a week.'

'That's gruesome,' I said. 'How come you don't have to work in the store too?'

'I can thank Carlos for that,' she answered. 'In fact, actually Steve, every time after I've boiled over about Carlos or at Carlos, I think about how he's saved me from that place, and I'm sorry for being so mean. See, Carlos is really quite a person. Even though he dropped out of school and gets along by hustling, everybody in the neighborhood respects him, and so do Mom and Dad; so when he said, "My little sister is going to go to a good school and study her books and not work in no damn *bodega*," there was a lot of screeching and bellowing, but in the end, that's how it turned out.'

'How does that go with his wanting you to be a virgin bride and mother at the age of eighteen?' I asked.

Sonia leaned back and gave me a mysterious smile. 'People are very complicated, Steve. You ought to know that.'

I nodded wisely and drained the last swallow of my drink. What a bummer to have to stop now, just when the conversation was humming along so easily and we felt so mellow. To my astonishment, I saw that Sonia was crooking a long, seductive finger at the waiter. He glided over and she gestured languidly at our empty glasses.

'The same, madame?'

'Please,' Sonia said.

My eyes popped, but I waited until he had gone to whisper, 'Have you got the moola?'

'My dear boy, I am certainly not going to wash dishes for this stuff, delightful though it may be.' Sonia gathered up the change from the first drinks and added a five. 'But that's it,' she said somewhat regretfully. 'And I've still got the train fare.'

The second two doubles had an even more remarkable effect than the first. We were even able to contemplate the airfield with equanimity, and the first thing we noticed was that now, close to ten o'clock, the activity was beginning to diminish dramatically.

'I wish we could stay really late,' Sonia said. 'I'd love to know how quiet it actually is along about three a.m.'

'We'd still be awfully conspicuous,' I objected. 'Maybe even more so.'

'There's got to be a way, Steve.'

'There will be. Don't worry. It's just going to take more time and planning than we had figured.'

'Well, patience isn't exactly my best feature,' Sonia said, 'but this is going to be worth it. We've got most of the facts now, disgusting as they are. The solution will come to us – maybe in a dream. Steve?'

'Mmmmm?'

'What are Will and Dorc going to say when we tell them how bad it is?'

'Screw Will and Dorc,' I said cheerfully.

'Maybe they should have come too, but I'm glad they didn't.' Sonia gave me a really melting look, and the martini began to run around like a mouse inside my head.

'Are you?' I croaked. 'Why?'

'Mmmm, because this is nice, just the two of us. Don't you agree?'

Normally I would have thought Sonia was playing with me and been really pissed off, but tonight it seemed perfectly natural and no more than my due. 'It is totally splendiferous,' I said firmly, and we beamed at each other.

'Let's start the mural right now,' Sonia said, 'while the old cadaver isn't looking.'

'No spray paint, alas,' I said, 'otherwise, whoosh!' and I pantomimed the first sweeping stroke at the wall. 'I wonder how far we could get before the waiter noticed what was happening.'

'For a while he would just stand there with that long jaw hanging down. Then he would start to jump up and down and gobble, and the manager would come running, and he'd jump up and down. Probably they wouldn't even try to stop us with their bare hands. They'd call the airport police. By the time they came, we could have done something quite spectacular.'

'But now you've come to the hairy part,' I said. 'Let's leave the airport police out of this pleasant evening.'

The waiter was coming our way again. He had the smug look of the menial who bears evil tidings. 'I regret. The bar is closing,' he said, without a shade of regret.

'Closing?' I said. 'The night is young.'

'Yes, sir. To you it may seem so, but there are few departures after ten o'clock.' He nodded towards the now desolate airfield and pocketed his tip without thanks. I had thought it quite generous, but probably we had been meant to pay more dearly for his disregard of the law.

'Never mind,' Sonia said graciously. 'We were just leaving.' She gathered herself together like a queen, and sailed out the door, while I marched along behind trying to look like a suitably impressive escort.

CHAPTER 9

Once outside the bar, we looked around and saw that the place was, indeed, dying before our eyes. Most of the ticket counters were closed, and the people who were still sitting or standing around had the forlorn look of those who should have been met but for some reason haven't been. It was enough to dampen the liveliest spirits, but I was determined to salvage what was left of the evening. The trouble was, I didn't know what to say that wasn't either depressing or idiotic. I settled for the briskly practical: 'Next we find the bus; it should be right outside this door.'

'Steve, this is depressing.'

'No, it's not. Look on the bright side. Imagine,' I said in a lower voice, 'that you are that lovely female languishing yonder. She has spent days deciding what to wear and, heedless of the cries and curses of the other passengers, the last hour of the flight in the bathroom working on her face – all this for her New York lover who has not shown up.'

This imaginative effort was like another martini for Sonia. She rallied visibly. 'The swine is in the pool hall,' she began, 'or thrashing about obscenely in some discotheque.'

'Or getting drunk with his wife at the country club,' I put in.

'No, that's too classy,' Sonia objected.

'My dear girl,' I said in my most private-school voice, 'you must never make the mistake of confusing country clubs with class.'

She chortled and gave me a hug. 'Steve, you're so funny when you go all WASPish. Do it some more.'

Luckily the bus was rolling up, which saved me from more of this tiresome impersonation. We were the only passengers except for two worker types, who were dropped off at another terminal, and it was impossible not to feel a bit somber as we passed through the vast, dark complexities of Kennedy Airport. There was so much of it, and it was all so hard to identify. Here and there we glimpsed the lighted tails of planes trundling around on their mysterious paths. Everything looked very lonely and deserted, but this, we had been assured, was pure illusion. These huge spaces were full of watching eyes, eyes that never slept because they were waiting for the likes of me and Sonia and Dorc and Will. I shivered and was glad when the bus pulled up at the oddly cheerful little station.

Again, we were in luck. There was a train waiting at the platform. An official-looking person took our money, gave us tickets, waved us inside and disappeared. Sonia glanced nervously around as we slid out of the station. 'How creepy,' she said. 'Do you realize we're the only people in this car – maybe in the whole train?'

I saw that she was right. We had the place to ourselves, and for a moment I had that nasty, prickling sensation down my spine which always accompanies the discovery that one is alone on a subway car. But this was the Train to the Plane, famous in song and story for being safe as well as clean. 'Don't worry,' I said. 'There's got to be a conductor, obviously, and I think a cop as well. These things are supposed to be incredibly safe.'

'First time I'll ever be glad to see one of those jerks,' Sonia muttered. She was still looking around dubiously and switching the end of her braid back and forth in her long fingers. A good deal of her natural ebullience seemed to have vanished, and her usually warm, golden skin had taken on a slightly greenish cast.

'You feeling all right?' I asked.

She nodded without too much assurance. 'Just very, very pooped,' she said. 'That was definitely a very pooping evening. I feel as if I could sleep for a month, non-stop.'

'Why not start now?' I said gallantly. I folded my cloak into a pillow and balanced it on my shoulder. Sonia gave a grateful little whimper and collapsed upon it. She had to bend quite a bit to get her head that low, but then bending into strange positions was one of her talents. I braced myself in the corner and gave what was left of my mind over to a kind of qualified rejoicing. For me the happier effects of the two martinis had not yet worn off. 'Watch it, boy,' I said to myself. 'From this height it's a long way down.' Basically I knew that Sonia was still Dorc's girl and that I was still good old, funny Steve, a treat to have around when you needed a laugh or a wacky idea, but sometimes rather a nuisance. I wasn't really fooling myself, but I was going to enjoy this train ride while it lasted.

After a while, the expected transit cop appeared from the car in front of ours. He gave us a remarkably benign look and said, 'How ya doin', kid?' and I grinned back at him silently, not wanting to waken Sonia with any inane banter. Still, it was nice to know that a friendly member of this usually hostile tribe existed, even if they kept him only for the Train to the Plane. He disappeared into the following car, and I was alone again with my increasingly heavy companion.

The train slid underground, and I tried to imagine the vast stretches of Brooklyn over our heads, Brownsville and Bedford-Stuyvesant, black ghettos far more frightening than Harlem, because they were so much less known. Up there people were trying to sleep four and five to a room or hanging out on corners wondering where to go, what to do. The street lights were shining feebly on broken windows and the blackened faces of burned-out buildings or on vacant lots where huge rats prowled through the rubble. I shuddered and tried to turn my imagination to better uses. Maybe Brooklyn wasn't there at all. Maybe the train had turned and gone out under the sea towards some shimmering green city beneath the waves. And I, a knight of the golden dolphin, was bringing a rescued princess of fabulous beauty home to my emerald halls.

The princess's head was breaking my shoulder by the time we stopped at Jay Street, and this was Brooklyn, close to home, and all too real. I gave Sonia a shake. 'Wake up, dear old cow,' I said. 'We have to get off in a minute.'

Sonia straightened painfully and looked around. Then she gave a disconsolate wail. 'Oh no, Steve. What you're trying to tell me is that we have to get up and stand in the subway for an hour and walk to the loft and tell Dorc everything and call Will and I don't know what else. I can't do it. I'm going to die right here and now.'

'No you are not. What would I do with the body? That's all I need. "Mystery death on Train to Plane. Teen art student held." You can die when we get to the loft and not a minute before.'

'You're not very sympathetic,' Sonia complained. I

thought this unfair in view of my aching shoulder, but the train was sliding into Broadway-Nassau now, and we struggled to our feet.

Subway stations late at night are like a bucket of cold water thrown over whatever warm, exciting or romantic experiences one may have had during an evening. You can come out of a party thinking how great your friends are, with the loud, hot music still beating in your head, and walk through the street feeling ten feet tall, but the sight of an empty subway platform is enough to crush the most soaring spirits. On this occasion we weren't in very good shape to begin with, and the effect was more than usually devastating. Sonia was hugging herself and looking more blue than green in the bleak light, so I put the faithful opera cloak around her shoulders and was rewarded with a wan smile. She looked extremely funny, but I managed to refrain from saying so.

Happily, the train wasn't too long in coming. We rode the short distance to Canal Street and trudged to the loft building in exhausted silence. I thought about the last time I had made this trek – the night the great idea had popped into my mind – and groaned to myself. It was all my fault. The days before I had had this unfortunate inspiration seemed golden in retrospect, carefree like the lost days of childhood. Now the damned idea sat on us like an incubus, draining our will to do or think of anything else.

CHAPTER 10

Like a recurring figure in a nightmare, Sylvia opened the door. She was wearing a paint-smeared dashiki, and her pale hair was a maze of little braids and beads. I was tempted to shove Sonia through the door and run for it, but this was not to be. 'Steve!' she cried delightedly. 'Give me five, man.'

'Ciao, Sylvia,' I said and gave her extended hand five perfunctory taps. Really this was too much. Dorc should do something about his mother.

Sonia was looking around helplessly. 'Where's Dorc?' she said. 'We've got to talk.' But when he appeared from the back of the loft, she merely folded up against his chest. 'Dorc, baby. It was awful. Put me to bed.'

Dorc raised his eyebrows at me while attempting to hold Sonia up off the floor. I nodded stoically. 'That about sums it up,' I said. 'Put the little lady down somewhere and come back.'

'I'll bring beer,' Dorc said succinctly, and led Sonia off towards the cube.

Sylvia was still standing there with an expression of bewilderment on her face. 'Now what have you young people been up to?' she asked in the light, cultivated tones of a mother in a drawing-room comedy. I was alarmed. Maybe the poor woman was schizo. This would account for a lot, but Dorc never seemed worried about her, so hopefully these aberrations were harmless.

'Oh, nothing much,' I said, 'just a really long and disgusting rehearsal at school.'

'Oh well then . . .' she murmured, and began to drift away. Obviously our problems impinged only very slightly on Sylvia's private world, and God knows, that was the way I wanted it.

Dorc appeared with two bottles of beer and beckoned me over to one of the giant bean-bags that served as furniture in his household. The sight of the beer sent a ripple of nausea through my system, but I decided to fake it. There were some aspects of the evening which I wanted to skate over lightly, and the two double martinis were among them.

'All right,' Dorc said when we had settled down. 'Tell.'

So I told, as briefly as I could get away with, the discouraging news from operation airport. Fortunately, it was all much as he had expected, so he didn't ask too many questions. When I had finished, he said, 'Well, so that's that.'

I took a cautious pull on my beer. Strangely, it didn't taste too bad. 'I'm not ready to quit,' I said. 'Something will turn up.'

'You're off your head. What's going to turn up? You mean you think some person or thing is going to come down from the sky and solve all the problems – some *deus ex* whatsit?'

'*Machina*,' I said automatically. 'Dorc, I don't know. Leave me alone. It's just a feeling I have, OK?'

'What about Sonia?'

'What do you mean what about Sonia?' I asked edgily.

'I mean, what does she think, moron?'

'Sonia's upset. She got over-tired.'

Dorc looked at me disbelievingly, as well he might. Nobody had ever seen Sonia over-tired. 'Why was she wearing that thing of yours?' he asked irrelevantly.

'She was cold,' I said. 'Was I supposed to let her catch pneumonia?'

'Well, it sure as hell looked funny.'

'Between here and Canal Street at this time of night, who cares? I was glad I had it.'

'How did your impersonation of a preppie come off? I see you managed to refrain from wearing even one button.'

'I was a smash hit,' I said. 'You'll see raves in all the papers tomorrow. But right now I have the delightful task of calling Will and telling him the bad news.'

'At this time of night? You must be mad. You'll get the judge.'

'I thought Will had his own phone.'

'He has his own extension,' Dorc explained patiently, 'and so has the judge. Right by his bed.'

'Terrific,' I said. 'Just what I need. But I promised to call as soon as we got in, whatever the time, so I don't see any way out of it.'

'Better you than me,' Dorc said. Nothing like a friend for encouragement in a tight spot.

I crawled wearily out of the bean-bag and over to the nearest phone which was conveniently installed in a hollow tree. Will's number seemed to ring forever, and I had just happily decided to hang up when a deep, angry voice said hello.

'Hello? May I speak to Will? I hope I didn't wake you up,' I gabbled.

'Young man,' came the terrible and by now unmistakable voice, 'you say you hope you didn't wake me. Would you have any idea just exactly what time of night it might be?' The judge spoke very slowly. He sometimes cultivated a black accent which, combined with his perfect diction, produced a curiously menacing effect.

'I'm sorry,' I said desperately. 'Will asked me to call him tonight. He said it was very important, and I couldn't do it before.'

'Would it be too much to ask your name before I rouse my son?' said the voice.

I was casting about wildly for a pseudonym when, to my intense relief, I heard Will's voice. 'I've got it, Dad. Hey, man, how did it go?'

'I won't go into detail now,' I said, listening in vain for a click from the other extension, 'but it wasn't at all good. In fact, it was shitty in the extreme.' I hoped the judge was still on the line. My language wouldn't shock him, but it might give a measure of offense.

'So it's all off?' Will said. 'There's no way we can do it?'

'Let's put it this way, Will. The problem of access is extremely difficult, but maybe not impossible. The problem of uninterrupted time looks really hopeless.'

The voice that came back to me over the phone was so depressed I wanted to cry. 'Man, Stevie, that is really a downer. I was counting on you two.'

'Well, you shouldn't have,' I said, more angrily than I had intended. 'Damn it, we all agreed before that it would probably be a waste of time, and now you're pissed off because we were right.'

Will sighed. 'Sorry, brother. I know you tried, and I'm sure you were great. I just hoped you'd turn something up, that's all.'

There was a sound of someone clearing his throat in a judicial manner, a sound not typical of my friend.

'Look, Will,' I said hastily, 'I really haven't given up. I'm still working on it, and I still think we'll come up with something. But let's talk tomorrow. I'm about to die. Call me around noon at the loft.'

'Good man. You'll be hearing from me,' Will said, and hung up.

I listened for a moment, but there was no second click. 'Sweet dreams, judge,' I said in my most mysterious voice and slipped the phone back on its cradle.

Dorc was still sitting there looking disgustingly fresh and fit, so I crawled back and took a few more slugs of my beer. It didn't seem to be doing me any harm, except for a creeping paralysis which was spreading gradually outward through my limbs. When it reached my fingers and toes, I felt that I would drop like a stone wherever I was, but the bean-bag seemed a safe place for this to happen. It would probably be my bed anyway.

'You were great,' Dorc said, presumably referring to my exchange with the judge.

'I know,' I mumbled. 'I'm just ever so funky.' I began to burrow into the bean-bag. It was really very comfortable, if only Dorc would get off the end so I could have it all.

'Well,' he said regretfully, 'I can see nothing more is going to be screwed out of you for a while. I'll let you sleep. Want a blanket?'

'No thanks. If I sleep in these clothes, they may look half-way decent by morning.'

'All right then.' Dorc got up and stood looking down at me. 'Flights of aardvarks sing thee to thy rest.' He slipped away through the dimly lighted shrubbery.

It was not, however, winged aardvarks which flapped through my dreams. I was visited instead by a slow phalanx of beautiful griffins. They came in out of a purple sky and settled gently onto the branches over my head, and there they sat gazing down at me with vast benevolence on their fierce, beaky faces. I suppose you could say, in the light of what finally happened, that my subconscious was trying to tell me something, but how even my subconscious could have known beats me.

It must have been nearly morning when I was awakened by the sound of a flute. I opened my eyes and saw that the lighting had changed. When I had gone to sleep, it had been merely peaceful and somber. Now, as if a late moon had risen, shafts of white light poured down through the branches. The music, which was extremely eerie in a pleasant sort of way, was coming closer, and at last I spied the musician. Dorc's father was strolling through his domain stark naked and playing the flute. Oh God, I thought, 'the piper at the gates of dawn', no less. As he passed my couch, he nodded his head up and down once in a grave and friendly fashion, without a pause in his playing, and passed on towards the other end of the loft. Compared with this my dream of encouraging griffins seemed like everyday reality, but I knew which was which all right. Giorgio Feltrinelli had been there in the all too evident flesh, with his little pot belly and his pointed beard, and the griffins were a figment of my imagination. He was playing out one of his little fantasies and, fond as I was of him, I was just as glad that this one didn't include me.

Before drifting off to sleep again, I had a couple of thoughts about the father figure which were more to the point. Here was a character, of immense resourcefulness and imagination, who almost certainly would not disapprove of our mad scheme. Maybe we should ask him for ideas. I would have to talk to Dorc in the morning, but on the whole I thought he would be against it. Dorc would say that his father's enthusiasm would be altogether too much, that he would get carried away and swamp us with wild and impossible schemes and then accuse us of being dull if we took a dim view. Still, I thought, the more ideas the better. We certainly weren't getting anywhere being sensible. At this point my tiredness took over, and I slept again to the sound of the distant flute.

As things turned out, I didn't get a chance to ask Dorc anything. My mother called at the shockingly early hour of eleven to ask me to come home. An old friend was arriving from Italy. She was delighted. My father was delighted. And if I wasn't delighted, I should come home anyway and act as if I were. In fact, I was still so nearly dead I could hardly remember who the marvelous visitor was, but it seemed easiest to do the familial thing and maybe get a chance to sack out again later in my own bed.

Sonia was still asleep, but Dorc was up and had made coffee which somewhat improved my outlook on life. 'Look,' I said, after I'd buried my face in a steaming mug for a minute, 'I've got to go home and play the dutiful son for a while. You talk to Will when he calls. You know everything that really matters. See if we can't all get together soon and try to get a new angle on this thing.'

'I'll see if we can all get together,' Dorc said, 'but let's get a new angle on something new, Steve. The whole plane thing makes me want to vomit.'

I was not surprised at his attitude, but the intensity of his feeling did take me aback. Probably it would be better not to argue for the time being.

'Well, we'll see when we meet,' I said. 'Thanks for the coffee anyway. It was cosmically refreshing. And now, farewell. Give Sonia regards from her munchkin lover.'

'What the hell do you mean by that?' Dorc shouted in a gratifyingly furious voice.

But I merely gave him what I hoped was an enigmatic smile as I wrapped myself once more in my cloak and faded toward the door.

CHAPTER 11

The friend from Italy proved to be delightful indeed, or would have been if I had understood any of his numerous languages. I had lost most of my Italian since our return and was far too tired to struggle with it. After a period of sitting around trying to look like an intelligent mute, I slipped thankfully away to my room and crawled under the covers. Some time later I was vaguely aware of my mother's voice saying that they were all going out to dinner and she hoped I could cope if I got hungry. I mumbled something affirmative and slumbered on.

By eight o'clock when the phone rang, I must have had almost enough sleep because I did hear it, and it had its usual electrifying effect upon me. Our phone is all the way out in the kitchen, but I had it on the third ring.

'Excuse me,' said the soft voice at the other end of the line. 'I wonder if I could speak to the Troll King?'

My God. I wasn't ready for this. I was still half asleep. 'Troll King speaking,' I said wildly. 'Griffin Man, is that really you?'

Silence. Maybe I had frightened him away. Then the voice spoke again in its gentle, lilting way. 'The one and only so far as I know. But you don't sound much like a troll – kingly or otherwise.'

'Oh no, I'm not. Not at all really. I'm an art student. I saw your griffin in the Canal Street station and well, hey, I just liked it so much I wanted to talk to you. So I put down my number and the first name that popped into my head.'

'Did you now?' the voice said in a gratified tone. Who, after all, is immune to a little flattery? 'Are you into griffins yourself then?'

'I've always liked griffins,' I said decisively, 'and wiverns and harpies and mandrakes and werewolves and all those folks.'

'Wiverns, now,' said Griffin Man. 'I don't believe I know wiverns.'

'They're a kind of little dragon. You'd like them. Look, why don't we meet someplace, and I'll show you one.'

The voice brightened noticeably. 'You'll have one with you?'

'Well, not in the flesh, but I'll draw you one, and I'll bring my bestiary. Have you ever seen a bestiary?'

'Not to my knowledge. Do I want to see one?'

'Absolutely. You'll get all kinds of great new ideas.'

'All right then. Statue of Alice.'

This was going too fast for me. 'Statue of Alice?' I said stupidly.

'You don't know the Statue of Alice?'

'Man, I'm a New Yorker born and bred.'

'So I'll meet you there tomorrow morning. I spend all my Sundays there.'

'Cosmic!' I cried. 'I'll be there. Wait a minute, though. How will I know you?' But Griffin Man had hung up. I stood there for a minute feeling baffled, wondering if I had dreamed the whole thing, but the kitchen light was glaringly bright, and I could feel a slight chill from the tiles creeping into my bare feet. I looked at the phone, but it just hung there on the wall, dumb and uninformative. After a bit, I padded back to my room shaking my head. He hadn't even said what time. Just that I should come in the morning. Well, I'd be there, maybe around eleven o'clock, just to be on the safe side. Probably among all the mothers and toddlers Griffin Man would be hard to miss. Since I was now thoroughly wide awake and rested, I decided to while away the rest of the night at my drawing board. A little practice on the old mythological beasts would not be amiss.

I snatched a few more hours of sleep along towards dawn, but the day when it came was too good to sleep through. I was ready to set off for Central Park well before the time I had set for myself.

CHAPTER 12

Travelers may rave about springtime in Paris or London or Rome, and I know what they mean, but for sheer, unadulterated joy on a fine April morning, you can't beat the old home town. Even a poor and ugly street, so long as there's one little tree putting out those new green leaves, seems to be brimming with unreasonable happiness. Central Park on such a day is overwhelming. It makes you want to get down on the grass and roll around, yelping like a puppy. I decided I would get off the subway at Fifty-ninth Street and check out the animals in the zoo to see how they felt about spring, before wending my way northward to Alice. Not surprisingly, they were all in their outside pens, looking fresh and wide awake and as yet unjaded by long hours of people-watching. I greeted the red fox, who had been one of my personal totems since childhood, and stopped for a few minutes to watch the seals at their joyous games. Then, with growing trepidation, I left the zoo and walked the short distance to the model-boat basin and the Statue of Alice. The boat basin provided another excuse to dally. Two beautiful, big sailing sloops were tacking back and forth in the fresh breeze, and I squinted to see if that intrepid mouse, Stuart

Little, might be at the tiller of one of them. No mouse. Only a couple of rather desperate-looking, middle-aged men, standing on the edge, watching their creations maneuver.

As I had guessed, it was easy to pick out Griffin Man once I had climbed the steps to the little plaza that surrounds the statue. For one thing, he was the only man in a bevy of smartly dressed mums and uniformed nannies who were watching, with varying degrees of apprehension, as their charges risked life and limb on Alice's shining, bronze extremities. Also, he had a drawing pad. Also, he was pretty weird looking. Although his clothes were perfectly normal – plaid flannel shirt, blue jeans – in other respects he fitted the name I had so randomly chosen for myself. Troll King, or maybe Dwarf King, would have suited him well. Not that he was really dwarfish in a grotesque way, but he was short and dark and alarmingly hairy. Now, I have grown up in a very hirsute time here in New York, but this guy was something else. He had an immense, untrimmed, black beard that hung down to his chest and a disordered mop of straight black hair that flopped down over a low forehead and nearly covered his eyes. In contrast, the hand that was busy over the drawing pad was small and white.

I edged over in front of him and stood looking down at another beautiful griffin drawing. This was probably intended as a signal, unless it was the only thing he could draw, which I doubted. After a moment, he raised his head. The eyes that peered out at me were astonishingly blue, and mild as the spring sky. For a long moment we simply gazed at each other, and I felt myself relax. I could deal with Griffin Man. We came, I felt sure, from the same place in the scheme of things.

At last he said, musingly, 'You don't look much like a troll either.'

I laughed and shook my head. 'More like a hobbit, I'm afraid.'

'Well, hey, you don't want to knock hobbits, you know.'

'Oh, I don't,' I said, 'but hobbit virtues are one thing and hobbit looks are quite another. You can't make it in this city with hair between your toes.'

'You'll make it all right,' he said. 'Do you have a proper name?'

'Steve Wiley when I'm at home.'

He held out his hand. 'Michael O'Leary at your service.'

'You're not, by any chance . . .?' I asked, shaking his firm, small paw.

He shook his head solemnly. 'Turkish on my mother's side, Chinese from the old man.'

'Sure Michael, and that's a lovely combination,' I said.

He gestured grandly to the spot beside him on the bench, and I sat. Next he produced a large thermos and two cups from a shopping bag at his feet. He poured two sizeable portions of what appeared to be orange juice, and handed me one. I took a good swig and reeled slightly. It was generously laced with vodka. 'Hey, Michael,' I said. 'It's a little early in the morning for me.'

'Never too early, my boy, and never too late either for that matter.' My new friend took a shockingly long pull on his juice and sat back with a contented sigh.

I peered down at the griffin. That Michael had an exquisitely accomplished hand was even more apparent in the pen drawing than it had been on the subway wall. And the style was strong and individual. It was not just a fine drawing; it was a drawing with a mind behind it. 'That's really super cool, Michael,' I said. 'Where did you learn to draw like that?'

'And where did you learn to draw?' he countered.

I gave the matter some thought. 'Well, in my room, I guess, and on the dining-room table and in the park and on the train and . . .'

'In short, on large quantities of plain white paper.'

'Mmmm. And some not so plain, like notebook paper and my mother's shopping lists and the margins of newspapers and so on. I have learned a lot in school, but I guess not the main thing.'

'Well, then it's the same with me, but no school.'

'Do you always do mythological beasts?'

'No, but I like them.' Michael started leafing through the pages of his pad far too quickly to satisfy my curiosity. 'I do dogs and little kids and other beasties just to keep my hand in. And sometimes, of course, I make things up.' He stopped at the portrait of a marvelously complicated being which seemed to have four wings and six heads.

'From space?' I asked.

'Or wherever,' Michael said, 'up above or down below, wherever you like,' and he waved his nearly empty cup in a sweeping gesture to include all of the universe, known and unknown.

I opened the bestiary, which had been lying in my lap, and started to show him the wonders it contained. He had obviously never seen anything of the sort before, and many of the creatures were new to him, though he did nod knowingly at some of the more obscure inventions of the Gaelic world.

'Steven,' he said, 'this is a wonderful thing. I could feed my mind for weeks on such a book.'

'Why don't you borrow it?' I said impulsively. 'We'll be meeting again. Keep it as long as you like.'

The blue eyes blazed out at me like sapphires from a dragon lair. 'You'd do that, truly? And we just met?'

'Without a qualm.'

'This calls for another drink,' cried Michael and poured his own cup full. There wasn't much room in mine, but he made the gesture anyway, and I did what I could to look grateful.

'Michael,' I said, after he had refreshed himself, 'why do you do graffiti? I mean, it doesn't seem just like you, and it's mostly kids who do it.'

'Graffiti?' he said in a slightly puzzled voice. 'Oh, wall drawings, like the one you saw. Well, maybe I want people to see my beasties sometimes. Why not? Besides that was a lovely piece of white tile, and I had a really good new marker, just the right size and in a perfect state of inkiness.'

I nodded appreciatively, but I still wanted to know more. 'You don't care it's against the law?' I asked. 'You could get caught, you know, and really be in deep trouble.'

'Screw the law,' Michael said with unexpected violence. 'What do I care for the friggin' law? A pox upon it and all its wormy branches.'

He looked really frightening now with his face screwed up and his eyes glaring out from behind all that hair.

'Easy, man, easy,' I said hastily. 'I was only asking what you thought about that sort of thing. I'm a graffiti artist myself, as far as that goes.'

'Are you now?' This mercurial person was all smiles again. 'You do those lovely great letters on the subway trains?'

I shook my head regretfully. 'No, Michael. I haven't been able to do one of those. You know those pieces are done by crews of Spanish and black guys, all jealous of their turf and all spoiling for a fight just on general principles. I mean, look at me, and look at that scene, and figure it out.'

Michael appeared to ponder this sad state of affairs with the utmost seriousness. 'So where have you managed to practice your art?' he asked finally.

'Well, I've done a big wall with some friends, and I've done the random little piece here and there – like your griffin – and, of course, I leave my tag around. I'm Sabre 75,' I finished with a touch of pride.

This was lost on Michael, however. He seemed never to have heard of me. 'I seldom ride the subway,' he said. 'The night of the griffin was an exception. My truck had been taken over by aliens.'

'Does this often happen?' I asked.

'Not often,' he said, 'which is why I know so little of the underworld.'

The idea of Michael as any sort of truck driver struck me as definitely bizarre. 'What kind of truck do you drive?'

'Just a small van, a catering van. I take supplies out to the airport and put them on the planes. It's not a thrilling job, but I get a lot of time to think, and then too . . .' His voice faded as he caught the look on my face. It must have worried him because he reached hastily for his thermos as if thinking to revive me from a faint.

'Michael,' I said in an awed voice, 'I am not a believer – not at all – but I think you've been sent.'

'Sent? Sent as in heaven sent?'

'Something like that.'

Michael took a pull on his drink. 'What makes you say that?' he said carefully.

For once words failed me. I stared around wildly, tried out my own drink, which had become warm and disgusting, and finally had a shot at it. I wasn't even sure at that point that I wanted to tell him about the plane, but it seemed inevitable. 'Well, it's hard to explain. I mean it's impossible to explain, but anyway I, that is we, you know my friends who did the wall with me, we were trying to think of a place to do a big graffiti piece, and well, we couldn't think of one, and then we thought – oh hell, Michael.'

He had been surveying me with an expression of mild wonder, and now he said calmly, 'So you thought of the airport.'

'Worse than that,' I said in a small voice.

A huge smile began spreading slowly under the beard. 'Dear Mary and Joseph and all the angels, you cocky little bastard. I have finally met my match for sheer, inspired looniness. You thought of an airplane, didn't you?'

I nodded speechlessly.

'Well, what's stopping you?' he roared suddenly. 'An idea like that should not be left to languish in the mind, my boy.'

'Now look,' I protested with some vigor. 'You of all people should know that you can't just go out on an airfield and paint a plane. It's impossible. We even went out to the airport and asked around, discreetly, of course, and everybody said the same thing. There is just no way you can get out on the field for any purpose for any length of time without all kinds of passes and clearances and God knows what.'

'But I can,' Michael said smugly. 'I and my little red van. We go there almost every night.'

'Well, that's what bowled me over, obviously, but somehow I can't feel that this solves all our problems. For one thing, if you help us, which you seem amazingly inclined to do, you could lose your job – probably would lose your job.'

'Screw the job,' Michael said predictably. 'But you're

right, it's not all plain sailing. How long does it take to do one of these things?'

'Hours,' I said gloomily.

'Hours, eh? Now that is a problem. We'll have to give the whole thing a fair amount of thought. Just let me mull it over a bit.' My improbable ally leaned back and lapsed into a deep silence. He applied himself again to his thermos and began to further disarrange his hair with one hand.

Meanwhile, I waited and worried. It was clear that I had started something, but what? And where would it all end? A vivid imagination can be more of a curse than a blessing, and in this department I was over-endowed. I could see the four of us squeezed between toppling stacks of toilet paper with our spray cans. Would there even be room? How could there be? In my imagination the truck was stopping at the gate to the airfield. Muffled voices. Mysterious thumps. They were going to search the van. It was like crossing the frontier of a hostile country, hidden under a bale of hay.

Michael, however, was coming out of his trance. 'Now then,' he said, 'let's assume for the moment that I can get you and your gang – how many did you say you were?'

'Four. And everyone but me is absolutely enormous.'

'Let's assume that I can get the four of you through the gate and onto the field. That should be no problem. I'll simply leave off some of the supplies and stick young artists in the empty spaces. Who cares if there's a shortage of Kleenex and toilet paper on flight one-twenty-seven?'

I thought quite a few people might care but held my peace, and he continued. 'You may be a little cramped, but great deeds are seldom done without a bit of suffering. The next problem is to get the right plane at the right time in the right place. For this you have to be ready.'

'Ready?' I said. He was moving too fast for me.

'Steven, when I find I am to service a plane that will be standing far out on the field, very late of a dark and stormy night, you and yours must be ready to move at extremely short notice. We'll have to establish a hotline.'

'Not too dark and stormy,' I said. 'We have to be able to see at least a bit, and I think the paint would run in a really lashing rain.'

'Moderately dark and threatening,' he amended. 'Then there's another problem you may not have thought of.'

'I doubt it.'

'Most of those super jets are too high to reach, man. What had you planned to do about that?'

'Ladders from somewhere around the airport?' I said hopefully. 'Little, rolling stair units? Don't they have those?'

Michael shook his head. 'Can't count on it. And that's one thing we can't squeeze into the van. It'll have to be one of the smaller planes.' He held up his hand when he saw my look of distaste. 'Nothing dinky, mind you. There are still some good-sized, intercontinental jets that are not impossibly high off the ground. Your tall friends could reach, and we'll pile up some boxes for the hobbit. You just have to rule out the jumbos. Be reasonable, man.'

It seemed to me that reasonable was about the last thing either one of us was being. 'All right,' I said. 'Fine. Now what about interruptions? What about having enough time?'

'Interruptions we'll have to leave to the good Lord,' he said, 'but choosing the right time and place will help a lot, and it seems likely that your experienced and resourceful driver could create some diversions. You must reconcile yourselves to working on the opposite side of the plane from the door where I will be bumbling to and fro, carrying out my appointed tasks with less than my usual not very great efficiency. Now don't worry about your masterpiece being seen,' he added after catching another look of disapproval from me. 'Planes turn around and about when they enter and leave an airport. It'll be seen, all right. Probably a lot sooner than you want it to be. As for time, I'll give you all I can – maybe even create some sort of disaster. How does a flat tire strike you?'

'As an attention-getting mechanism.'

'Not necessarily. Who wants to help an idiot like me change a tire at three a.m. on a nasty night? But one thing I must most ferociously urge upon you and your cohorts and that is speed. Speed, speed, speed!' he shouted, jumping up and glowering down at me. 'You must be swifter than the dragon's tongue. Your spray cans must descend upon that plane like a hurricane and depart. Do I make myself clear?'

'Clear is what you make yourself,' I said, trying not to cringe under this onslaught, 'but, you know, it has to be a good job. We're not going through all of this just to make a mess, and a good job takes time.'

'You'll have to practise,' he answered sternly. 'You'll have to depart from the tradition of spontaneity which seems to characterize these affairs. I have heard that some of your subway-car artists plan what they're going to do ahead of time. You'll have to do better than that. You'll have to actually execute your design over and over again. With a stop-watch. How do you like that?'

'I don't like it,' I said, 'but I see your point, and none of us would mind doing it if we had a place to do it in.' I stopped and thought, and Michael subsided again beside me. There was, of course, an obvious solution, and I remembered how recently I had wondered if Dorc's father might play a role in our enterprise. One of the bigger walls of the loft would serve the purpose nobly, and we would have peace and quiet and plenty of beer. The only question was whether even the father figure would be willing to sacrifice a whole wall to endless layers of spray paint. On further reflection I thought I could probably find an approach that would hook him. I could feel excitement building up inside me, but now Michael was beginning to look depressed. Probably I had raised too many objections to what was, after all, an extremely princely offer on his part. 'OK,' I said decisively. 'That's cool. I've thought of a place, Michael. And don't worry about our working hard. That's no problem. When we get through, we'll be so fast all you'll see is a blur, but I still don't know what the time will be. We haven't even designed the thing yet, so let us get at it, and when we've gotten as fast and as good as we can, we'll invite you to a performance. Then we can make our final plans.'

I was pleased to see that I had restored Michael's joy in life. He was beaming again, and he held out his hand which I shook ceremoniously. 'Praise the Lord!' he cried. 'I was afraid you'd gone all practical on me.'

'Heaven forbid,' I said.

'Down with practicality!' he answered, and we drank to that.

I wrote down Michael's phone number and promised to call and give him a progress report in about a week. Then, after another handshake and a few more words of mutual admiration, I dashed away to find a telephone and call the loft. I didn't know how I was going to get Giorgio Feltrinelli alone, but this seemed like a minor hurdle and one which I must jump as soon as possible. At the edge of the boat pond I turned and waved to Griffin Man, where he sat under the benign gaze of Alice, and he waved back with glorious abandon.

CHAPTER 13

There was no answer at the loft. I stood still for a minute thinking about the fact that it was now only a little after noon on a Sunday. Probably they were all asleep and had turned the telephone bell off, an annoying habit which I knew they had. It was no good just standing around in my present state of mind. I would have to go there and break the door down.

The park was filling up, becoming its wondrous Sunday patchwork of colorful people, as I angled across to Columbus Circle to catch the A train. The cat man was there with his six pug-faced Persians indolently draped over their little bicycle-drawn carriages. A steel band was setting up at a busy corner and, at a suitable distance, an improbable classical trio of tuba, oboe and viola da gamba was already in business. Normally I would have been happy to spend the day drifting from one curious outdoor event to another, but today I gave them only an appreciative glance.

It was well after one when I reached the door of the loft, and I knocked with the righteous firmness of one who has been up for hours and accomplished great things while others slept.

To my relief, it was Giorgio who came to the door. At this point I hadn't the patience to deal with any of Sylvia's manifestations. He was barefoot and tousled but seemed fairly normal – but not too normal, I hoped, because when he was actually working hard on something, he became as hard to get to as any busy adult. I needn't have worried, for he ushered me in with a gesture of exaggerated courtliness.

'Sir Steven!' he cried. 'Be welcome and thrice welcome to this humble hall. Know that in our royal exile our heart is glad to greet our most valiant and far-ranging knight.'

I dropped to one knee, hoping for inspiration. 'Greetings, oh wise and puissant lord,' I said. 'I have a weighty boon to ask.'

'Arise, most honored knight. The boon is yours. We'll lift a cup of cheer together while we hear of it.' Giorgio moved off toward the refrigerator while I trailed dubiously behind. The sight of a gallon jug of wine made my eyes cross slightly. I like a drink as well as the next teenager, but it seemed to me that the adult world had lately been conspiring to keep me sloshed twenty-four hours a day. Giorgio waved me into a bean-bag, poured for both of us, and settled down with an expectant look. 'And now your boon that I may grant it,' he said.

'You'd better hear it first,' I answered, trying to lead the way into a somewhat less exhausting conversational style. 'Giorgio, I need a wall.'

He regarded me gravely. 'A wall. "I need a wall," quotha. What kind of a wall, if I may ask? A garden wall? A defensive wall? A convent wall? Or will any kind of wall serve your mysterious purposes?'

'A plain, white, indoor wall. Like that one,' I said, pointing to a vast expanse that glimmered behind the tree trunks. 'Dorc and Will and Sonia and I: we need a big wall to practice a, er, mural on. It's something we're doing someplace else, but we need to get it right in privacy, not being all that experienced at this sort of thing, if you know what I mean.'

'And suppose I don't like this, er, mural?' Giorgio asked in a distressingly practical voice. 'After all, I have to live and, what is more important, work in this space. Suppose you produce something which quite shatters my artistic vibrations. What then?'

'Oh, we'll paint it out,' I said hastily. 'Don't worry. It'll be as good as new.'

There was a pause, and from a branch over my head the parrot gave a sudden, harsh laugh. I wished I had something to throw at it, but that might have antagonized Giorgio. He, for his part, got up and strolled over to the wall. He looked at it thoughtfully from several angles, and then he nodded his head. 'Well, why not?' he said. 'That space has been taunting me for some time now – just begging to be ravished, you might say. Besides, never let it be said that I, of all people, stood in the way of, etcetera, etcetera. Paint away.'

'Giorgio,' I cried. 'You are really a cosmically wonderful guy. We thank you from our very bottoms and all that.'

I felt a little guilty about not disclosing the true nature of our work, but thought once it was under way, he probably wouldn't mind. Only one thing still worried me, and it was far from minor. I knew from using just one can of spray paint rather briefly in a closed room that the effect on the atmosphere was catastrophic. Even the high which was the first symptom of breathing these fumes was not much fun, and it was followed by headaches, sometimes nausea, and who knew what other disgusting reactions. The loft, of course, was immense, but so was our project. If all four of us spray-painted in there for several hours, the place would become uninhabitable. I glanced at the windows and felt slightly reassured. Unlike the windows of many lofts, these apparently did open, and open wide. I would pray for warm weather and for greater tolerance from the elder Feltrinellis than I had any right to expect. Meanwhile, I must press forward and leave these cowardly speculations to some other time when they would surely return to haunt me.

I sprinted across the loft and pounded on the door of the cube. Sounds of hostility were heard within. 'Dorc!' I shouted. 'Wake up, you ten-toed sloth. I've got great news.'

The door was jerked open, and Dorc stood there glowering and rumpled. 'It better be good,' he said. 'For Christ's sake, you weasel. I was up all night.'

I had been through this before and was undaunted by his murderous visage. 'It's the best, the breakthrough. Dorc, I've found a way to do the plane. I've found someone who can help us.'

Dorc stood there for a moment swaying slightly. Then he slid backwards into his bed. 'Get me some coffee,' he croaked, 'and then say it all again.'

I sighed and trekked out to the kitchen. I had been through this before, too, so it didn't take me long to get the kettle on and find the emergency supply of instant coffee. I was also prepared for the complaints I would get because I hadn't brewed a fresh pot. This was no time for gourmet sensibilities, and the storm would gradually rumble away as my friend revived. On second thoughts, I made a cup for myself, thinking to counteract the various potions which had been poured down my innocent throat in the past few hours. In fact, I had never felt brighter, but there might be a backlash effect in store.

After the predicted amount of grumbling and sipping, Dorc sat back and listened to my tale with his usual intense concentration. I could practically hear the wheels going round in his head as he probed for weaknesses and tried to keep his own excitement in check. Weaknesses, of course, would not be hard to find with a far dimmer mind than Dorc's, but I could see his eyes begin to glow and his mouth to twitch with delight as I described Griffin Man and his amazing proposal. Cynicism was going to come hard on this occasion, and, in fact, he didn't even try it on. Instead he reached for a pad and pen. 'Fantastic,' he mumbled, as the long body of a plane began to take shape on the white page. 'Really incredible, Steve. And not least getting the father figure to lend us a wall. I couldn't have done that.'

'You're his son,' I said. 'That makes a difference. Besides, we have a sort of rapport.'

Dorc nodded, not unkindly. 'Two weirdos from the same asylum. What did we agree to write?'

'We didn't,' I answered, 'and I've got to call Will and Sonia right now – get them over here if possible. You free this afternoon?'

'I am now,' Dorc said. I could see big rounded letters, first a 'P' then an 'E' then an 'A', taking shape as I reached for the telephone.

CHAPTER 14

To my surprise, we were all assembled by four o'clock. I thought of Michael's suggestion that we have a hotline, and hoped that it would work as well when the crucial moment came.

Will was wearing a powder blue, pin-striped suit and a black top hat, and he had a fifth of Chivas Regal clutched under his arm, the sight of which made my stomach do one complete somersault before coming to rest again. 'I thought this called for a little formal celebration,' he said solemnly. Then he gave a huge smile, threw the bottle and the hat on the bed, and spread his arms wide, as if to embrace all of us in the little room. 'My friends,' he began again, 'this is an historic occasion. From this day forth . . .'

But now Sonia interrupted by throwing her arms around Will. 'Will, darling. No speeches. I'm too happy to listen to a speech, even one of your gorgeous ones. Steve!' Now it was my turn to be mauled. 'We've got to thank Steve. Without him none of this would ever have happened.' Sonia, in jeans and a bright red shirt, looked as if a bonfire had been lit inside of her.

I wriggled free and held up a restraining hand. 'Let's

save the bouquets for when it's actually done,' I said. I tried not to sound too repressive, but Sonia gave a wail.

'Does somebody always have to be a wet blanket? Can't we all be optimistic together, just once?'

'Sure, Sonia. Come on. I didn't mean to be depressing. I just wanted to point out that we've got a lot to do. Somebody get some glasses and ice,' I added bravely.

When we had all settled down with variously mixed glasses of scotch, Dorc pulled out the paper he had started when we were alone. 'You know how it is,' he said. 'Natural, nervous reaction – have to get something down on paper. I don't know whether we're going to go with this "peace" idea of Sonia's or not . . .' He passed around the sketch he had done of the big plane. It had both "peace" and "*pace*" written on it in different graffiti styles.

For once Sonia, wisely I thought, kept her mouth shut, and we all looked at Will. With a feeling of relief I realized that he would surely turn out to be the operational chief of the enterprise. He had the right kind of charisma for the job and an organizational sort of mind. In fact, we were all leaders, which made us a tricky bunch to lead; but Will was the natural choice. Of this, I might add, he was well aware. 'I said it was good, way back there in the pits,' he said. 'I also said it was terrible, but that was before I had a chance to think about it.'

'It still makes me squirm a bit,' Dorc said. 'While I was doing this doodle, I still felt just a tad embarrassed, you know.'

'Oh don't be so intellectual, Dorc.' (This was Sonia, of course.) 'Anyway, have you got a better idea?'

'Not really,' he admitted. 'What about you, Steve?'

'I like it. I like its design possibilities. And you know,

we can put our names inside the big letters. Without tags it wouldn't be New York graffiti.'

'Everyone for peace, then?' Will said, and we all nodded.

We passed from this general agreement to discussion of which languages and alphabets to use with me holding out hard for Greek and Arabic over the others' objections that these languages would be totally obscure to most people. In the end I had my way, after I pointed out that while we couldn't really choose our plane on the basis of where it was going, routes including Athens and one of the Arabic-speaking countries were fairly common. Greek lettering, I added, was attractive, and it was an old universal language, even if hardly anybody but Greeks spoke it any more. Russian was an obvious contender in the strange alphabet field, but I said that planes usually made a direct jump from here to Russia and that besides, I had looked up the Russian word for peace along with the others and hadn't liked the look of it. Next we thought about '*pace*' and decided that even though Italy was a logical stop on our imaginary itinerary, we would go for the Spanish word instead, Spanish being the language of many New Yorkers and other inhabitants of the western hemisphere. It seemed like more of a two-way communication if we used Spanish. So this is what came out of the battle of the languages:

PEACE PAZ εἰρήνη سلام

'But what the hell does it say?' Dorc asked, peering at the Arabic letters.

'It says "peace" in Arabic, of course,' I answered smugly.

'I know that, you twit, but it must have a sound of some sort.'

'Ah, you're asking what the transliteration is. Now I see the problem.'

'Come off it, Steve.'

'It says "*salaam*",' I said, relenting. 'Isn't that cool? It's the word people use to greet each other all over the Middle East, but it also means just plain peace, as in "make peace, not war". See why I like it? And the Greek letters, in case you ignorant slobs can't read them either, come out "*irini*" – something like the girl's name.'

'I propose that we give the Arab word to our little language scholar,' said Will. 'Consider it a reward for all your sterling services.'

He probably meant it as a punishment for priggishness rather than a reward, but if so, it back-fired since this was the one I had wanted all along. The flowing Arabic script fascinated me. I could only wish it didn't have that nasty little '*mim*' symbol way out there by itself at the left end, but there was nothing I could do about that. The other words were also fairly easy to parcel out. Sonia got '*paz*', not so much because she is Spanish as for the shortness of the word. It would give her time and space to do some of the creepy floral embellishments which were her specialty. Will got 'peace', because it seemed to suit his big, rounded graffiti style, and Dorc was happy to be left with the Greek. He was, after all, the only one of us who really liked lettering for its own sake, and this would be a challenge.

From this point we passed to the first stages of the actual design. 'It would look great in a square, two above and two below with nice, bulgey borders,' I said, 'but we'd better stick to putting them all in a row. The problem of reaching high enough is going to be horrendous as it is.' Dorc gave everyone paper and pens, and silence fell. We worked and worked, our drinks largely forgotten at our elbows. No one even thought to put on any music, which was probably just as well. Even in a group as close as ours, music can be a source of conflict. We were totally content.

I won't go into detail about the period we spent designing our big piece. It was very exciting to us but wouldn't be to anyone else, not even to another artist. Besides, these things are hard to put into words. Farther on into the evening Dorc did put on some records which met with at least qualified approval from everyone. By this time he had also put a big rack of design markers in the middle of the floor, and we were working in color. You can simulate the effects of spray paint pretty well with markers if you know how. At one point we crawled out to the kitchen for some munchies and came back with a big pot of coffee. Finally Dorc pinned a long sheet of paper to his drafting table, and we took turns putting our creations down in carefully measured spaces. The result was four great pieces in a row, but we were too tired to think of a way to give them unity.

'Tomorrow, right after school,' Will said, 'we'll come here, and we'll solve this problem. We'll sleep on it, and it will go away. Meanwhile . . .' He stopped, and an expression of total consternation came over his face. It would have been funny, if it had not been so alarming. 'Meanwhile,' he repeated very slowly, 'someone has got to think of a way to buy an immense load of spray paint.' It was amazing, as I look back on it, that even Will could have forgotten this decidedly sticky problem. There had been talk of a war chest in the beginning, but nothing had been done about it. Somehow, I think we had all assumed that once the more exotic obstacles began to yield, the prosaic question of finance would miraculously be answered. Probably it would be more accurate to say that we just hadn't thought. We had been too carried away.

The problem of money was not trivial. Nor could it be dealt with by simply begging a little extension here and there of our normal allowances or expenses or whatever our various families chose to call their handouts. At more than three dollars a can for spray paint, a big piece would cost thirty to forty dollars, and what we were proposing to do was a big piece over and over again. In the folklore of graffiti, the artists are supposed to 'rack up', or steal, their paint, thereby further showing their contempt for the establishment. Like many colorful customs, this one has its feet planted firmly in economic nitty-gritty. Graffiti art is an expensive pastime.

Theft, I should add, was out of the question in this case. Not only had our middle-class lives disabled us morally for such an operation, it was also just plain impossible in a short period of time to steal the amount of paint we needed. We'd have had to hold up a hardware store with sub-machine guns.

'I hate to think what this is going to cost,' I said. 'My mind boggles and my stomach turns.'

'A couple of hundred,' Will said, 'and I ain't got it, my friends, just in case you were thinking I might.'

We looked at each other in appalled silence, our minds racing futilely around among various hare-brained schemes for getting rich quick.

Sonia, who was sitting cross-legged on the floor, put her face in her hands in a sudden gesture of despair, and we all looked at her. When she raised her head, her expression was haggard. 'Oh God,' she said, 'I'll get the stupid money. Nothing could be simpler. I'll do a job for Carlos.'

Dorc was on his feet in a flash and towering over her. 'Oh no you won't,' he shouted. 'Over my dead body.'

'Don't be an idiot, Sonia,' I added. 'That's beyond the call of duty or anything else.'

Sonia jumped to her feet blazing with fury. 'Shut up, all of you,' she cried. 'I'll take my own chances, and I'll do what I want to get what I want. What do you know about it? You're children, all three of you.'

Will came over and put his big hands on her shoulders. 'The problem is, dear Sonia, that we are not children, and we do know something about it, and you are not, I repeat *not* going to run any drugs for Carlos and get thrown in the slammer. What, may I ask, would happen to our great creation then? It would be minus a very important piece, and we would be minus a very important girl. Do I make myself clear?'

Sonia squirmed impatiently during this appealing speech, but you could see that she was softening. 'Don't be ridiculous, Will,' she said, but in a milder tone. 'It's not all that dangerous. I know people who do it all the time. I just always thought it was ugly, and I never wanted money enough to fool around with drugs.'

'No,' Dorc said.

Sonia turned on him. 'Don't tell me what to do, Dorc. I'm warning you.'

Dorc said softly, 'Sonia, I promise never to tell you what to do or what not to do again, if you just don't do this one thing.'

'Darling, I'm telling you it's no problem,' Sonia said. She seemed to be torn now between exasperation and affection. 'I won't sell anything. I'll just make a couple of long deliveries. Little kids are rolling in money just from getting in a cab at one place and getting out at another.'

'And walking straight into the arms of the law which

isn't quite as stupid as some people think,' Will said. 'No, you lovely, brave wench. Just let me think a minute. There's got to be another way.'

Sonia subsided, and we all went back to beating our brains. In point of fact, she wasn't the only one who could take this dubious road to wealth. I knew a guy who would give me an errand to do any time I asked. He thought I was perfect. Who would suspect a little innocent like me? Answer: A lot of people. Anyway, like Sonia, I had never wanted money that badly, and given my financial ups and downs, you can judge how much I really didn't want to run any drugs. I think we all felt the same, and maybe Sonia the most of all. It wasn't even the horrible prospect of getting caught that turned us off. It was drugs, period, and what they did to people. I could tell myself endlessly that if I didn't do it, someone else would, so what difference did it make, but the answer was always the same. Negative.

It was a rotten situation, and naturally Will was the one who finally bailed us out. He suddenly started grinning, and I think he was genuinely pleased with the idea he had, although it must have been a painful one. 'I've got it,' he said. 'I know something I can sell. Don't worry, I'll never miss it, and it should do the trick. You all get started tomorrow, sketching in the lines, and I'll be along as fast as I can with the paint.'

We were mystified but relieved, and it wasn't until Tuesday, when Will borrowed Dorc's clock to time our work, that we realized his heavy gold watch was gone.

Having solved what seemed at the time to be the last major problem, we parted, feeling washed out but serene.

It occurred to me as I climbed the last flight of stairs to our apartment that I had never been so tired before in my life. It was after one o'clock, and tomorrow was a school day, and after school, another design session, and then school again and so on. Somewhere in that schedule something was going to have to give a little so I could get some sleep. Maybe I would cut school one day, but not tomorrow, when I had a social studies test. For a frightening moment it seemed as if I had not only forgotten what the test was about, but also the subject of the entire unit we were supposedly studying. Oh yes. China. The story of 4,000 years cleverly compressed into one week for the enlightenment of New York youth. Presumably, it would all come back to me when I sat down to take the test. It usually did. Unless I passed out first.

In the bathroom, I gloomily surveyed my hair. It was, in my view, disgustingly dirty, which was not surprising, since I came to the same conclusion every night of my life. From time to time my mother was foolish enough to suggest that I could let it go a day. She always got snarled at for her pains. I didn't enjoy washing my hair every day, but I wouldn't go out for anything like this. Well, maybe if Griffin Man called and said it was D Day. I'd probably want to wear a black hood or something of the sort on the big night. A little shiver of apprehension went up my aching spine as I padded off to my parents' room. I took the alarm clock back into the light, set it for five thirty, so I could wash my hair in the morning, put it back and whispered the usual few words to my half-awake mother. Then I threw myself on my bed expecting to be dead on contact.

No such luck. As so often happens when one has been concentrating fiercely on one thing, the damn graffiti piece wouldn't let me sleep. The letters kept forming and reforming in my head, first in black and white, then in vivid and increasingly psychedelic colors. Now they were swelling to an incredible size. I was standing on my toes with a spray can in my hand, straining to reach, as the top of my Arabic *alef* grew by itself, up and up into the darkness. I absolutely could not reach so high. I stepped back with a cry of despair and then was suddenly swept with a great feeling of relief. If it wanted to paint itself, that was cool. Let it go its way and I could sleep.

CHAPTER 15

To say that we worked hard that week would be like saying that the ceiling of the Sistine Chapel was really a lot of bother for Michelangelo. Well, maybe that's not the best comparison I could have thought of. Anyway, it was a week to remember. The idea that kids are lazy is based on a misunderstanding of what work is all about. The only projects we don't work hard on are the ones other people think up for us to do. That week we went to school from eight to three and worked at the loft from about four until nearly midnight, with a few short breaks here and there to stoke the furnace. Will made an excellent slave driver, and one could see that he enjoyed it. 'You're draggin' yore ass, boy,' he would shout, waving his own spray can menacingly if one of us flagged, and the offending party would shout back, 'Yes, massa! Coming, massa!' This is not to say that Will didn't work like a demon himself. In fact, between being timekeeper and whip-cracker, and doing his own large part of the piece, he was busier than any of us.

As Will had predicted, the basic problem of unifying the design yielded quite promptly on Monday afternoon, and we spent the rest of that day laying it out in pencil, first on paper, next on the wall itself. When we began working out in the loft, I kept looking over my shoulder to see if Giorgio was standing behind me thinking evil thoughts about the nature of our 'mural', but Giorgio seemed to have completely disappeared. This unexplained absence bothered me, and I finally asked Dorc what had become of his father. 'Oh, he's lighting an off-off-Broadway show somewhere,' Dorc said. 'Working day and night. Nice to have him out of our hair, isn't it?'

I agreed, but continued to wonder at the mysterious ways of the father figure. A sudden call to light a play? Well, maybe. In any event it was one less person to be asphyxiated when we started to paint.

Sylvia drifted through from time to time wearing an intriguing assortment of costumes, but she seemed to be living, even more than usual, in a world of her own. Except for the ever more furious pace at which we drove ourselves, it was a peaceful scene.

By Tuesday we were actually spray-painting with the gorgeous arsenal of colors Will had bought. As if, improbably, the gods approved our project, the weather had turned unusually warm for April, so we flung wide the windows of the loft, letting the winds of spring sweep through the branches of the jungle and carry away the worst of the aerosol fumes.

The first attempt took us from five o'clock, when Will blew a police whistle and shouted 'Go, you bastards!' until ten, when he blew it again and announced in a much more subdued voice, 'I think this one is finished, my friends.' We had eaten and peed first, so the work had been almost uninterrupted. It still took five hours, and the finished product, while exciting, left much to be desired. We stood around mopping our brows and gazing at it with a mixture of pride and disgust. Dorc produced some beer, and a reluctant post mortem began. We had agreed at the beginning that we had to do two things at the end of each pass. One was to criticize the quality, and the other was to paint it out so the wall would be ready the following day. Needless to say, of these two tasks the first was preferable.

'One thing is obvious,' Will said, when we had finished pointing out the defects in the painting. 'There is one obvious, simple way to pick up speed, and that is to help each other at the end. Naturally, some people work faster than others, and this is no reflection on their artistic genius. Also, I suppose some parts of this thing may be a little easier – no, make that a little less time-consuming – than others. Steve was diddling at the end, putting in little refinements, and so was I. We have to know each other's designs well enough to help finish them, and no chauvinistic snapping and snarling, please, when someone moves over to help fade an edge or fill in the background. Right?'

We nodded wearily. It was, as he said, obvious and not even particularly distasteful. Graffiti artists often work in each other's territory, if they are a team to begin with. Dorc was looking the most discouraged. I think he has less stamina than the rest of us, and he was also maybe a shade more intelligent when it came to assessing the odds for success. 'Five hours,' he groaned. 'My God. How long did your weird friend say we could have, Steve?'

'He didn't say,' I answered. 'He's not a very specific person, I'm afraid, and besides, he really doesn't know. He just gave me a lot of stuff about forked lightning, speeding bullets, flickering dragon's tongues – a bunch of horribly hasty metaphors.'

'Big help,' Dorc said. 'Good God. The blind leading the blind.'

It was time for a shot of leadership, and Will was ready for us. 'Now hold on a minute,' he commanded, 'and listen to me. You have no idea from this first attempt – you have, in fact, not the smallest clue – how fast we can work. Tomorrow we will cut at least an hour, I promise you, and after that it will go faster every time.'

Sonia was chewing the end of her braid, not, I am happy to say, one of her usual mannerisms. 'I think it would help if we doodled it all the time when we're not here.'

'Run that by me again,' Dorc said.

'Don't be dense,' Sonia answered impatiently. 'You know what I mean. When we're in class or on the train or something, we should be sketching our design over and over so that when we're actually painting we won't have to hesitate for even a second trying to think what comes next.'

'Not for me, thank you, my dear. I dream the damn thing all night and practically eat it. I'm not in the least danger, I assure you, of forgetting what comes next.'

'Well, maybe we're not all quite so brilliant,' Sonia said nastily, and Will raised a massive paw.

'Quiet, children. There shall be no squabbling, particularly not lovers' squabbling.' He glared at Sonia and Dorc, and they glared back. 'Didn't I say that everyone works differently?' he went on. 'What bores one person out of his skull may be just the thing for someone else.'

'I don't mind the idea,' I said. 'I'm going to try it, and if it starts to drive me round the bend, I can always stop.'

'All right then,' Will said, ignoring the still baleful glances of Dorc and Sonia. 'Now to make this glorious mess as white as driven snow.'

Groaning and cursing, we picked up cans from the ample supply of white spray paint and applied aching arms to the task of obliterating our work.

CHAPTER 16

During the following days we worked hard, quarreled little, and picked up an astonishing amount of speed. The one thing we didn't do was to discuss at any time the viability of the whole idea. I don't really know why. I know that I, at least, took time to entertain the gravest doubts. This, perhaps, was because I had met Michael O'Leary and the others hadn't. I kept thinking in particular of the vast amounts of vodka he had tossed down on a Sunday morning. Surely this was not the best omen? Suppose he over-fortified himself when it came to the crunch? Suppose it was all an alcoholic fantasy and the crunch never even came? Suppose this. Suppose that. But then, worry is a way of life with me. If I didn't have anything to worry about (and who could possibly say I didn't?), I would invent something. For the others, I think Michael and his magic van served as something more than just a practical solution to a practical problem. In that role he certainly left much to be desired. Instead, I think he was a catalyst. We had been like a long simmering pot. Throw in a pinch of Michael, and we were suddenly on the boil. However all that may be, during those days nobody had the bad taste to say, 'What if it doesn't work?' or, 'Now come on, how are we really going to bring this off?' We had our hands full with the specific problem of speed, and the final result was truly remarkable.

One hour and twelve minutes on Saturday night. Beyond that we felt sure we could not go, and Giorgio's wall was beginning to look distinctly pregnant. We stood back and looked at each other and at our piece. It was really beautiful. If we could do even half as well in the new and difficult conditions of the airfield, the result would be worthy of the most discriminating international audience. 'Let's not paint it out this time,' I said. 'Maybe when the father figure actually looks at it, he'll want to keep it for a while. After all, it can't be much of a secret by now.'

Dorc laughed. 'He's a deep one,' he said, which seemed to sum up both his father and their relationship.

'So what do we do now?' Sonia asked. 'I'm feeling impatient and scared all at the same time.'

'First we rest,' Will said, 'all day Sunday, like the Lord after the creation. Then I guess Steve had better call Michael and tell him it's green for go. We wouldn't want him to pass up any opportunities, thinking we weren't ready. On the other hand, you all know I am sure that we're going to have to wait, and that is going to be the worst thing we have been through yet.'

'We'll lose our edge if it takes too long,' Dorc said, 'not to mention our nerve.'

Sonia turned to me. 'Steve, do you think we should have a meeting with Michael, show him the piece, let him see what the rest of us are like?'

I said that I would ask him when I called but that somehow I didn't think so. Michael was shy in a funny sort of way. Not that he was afraid to talk to people, but he might not relate to everybody. I had a feeling that in his mind my friends were only extensions of me, sort of like extra hands that I would use to accomplish my ends. My ends and his, I thought, and then doubts assailed me again. I sure as hell hoped Michael was still with me. If not, all this ghastly work would have been for nothing, and the other three would probably put me to some truly revolting death. Naturally, I did not express any of these horrible thoughts in words. I just said I'd call Michael and let them know what transpired.

Miraculously there were a few inches left in the Chivas Regal bottle, which either shows how virtuous we had been all week or that we didn't really like scotch very much. Dorc brought some glasses from the kitchen and divided it up so that we could toast each other and our creation. In our condition, the neat whisky was just short of lethal, but it didn't matter. All we had to do was get to our various beds and stay there if need be until Monday morning.

CHAPTER 17

It was Sunday evening before I had the energy and moral fortitude to call Griffin Man, and even then I dialed his number with a sinking feeling in my stomach. 'Michael? This is Steve.'

'Ah, Stevie, me lad!' The voice was overflowing with joviality, but somehow I had the distinct impression that he didn't know who I was.

'The Troll King,' I said. 'The New York hobbit.'

'Ah, *that* Stevie! The owner of the wonderful book. The painter of planes. The scourge of the MTA.'

'The very one,' I said, still not feeling so reassured as I might have been. 'And it's about the plane I'm calling you, Michael. We've practised like fiends all week, and we're ready to do the deed whenever you are.'

'Are you, begorra?' he cried, the brogue now pronounced to the point of parody.

I ground my teeth. It seemed to me that the last thing we needed out in that cold, hostile place was a leprechaun. 'Michael,' I said sternly, 'remember your Turkish mother and your Chinese father.'

Michael sounded deeply aggrieved. 'Would you be putting down the Irish, me boy? We can't have that, you know. Sure and that would be a sorry thing.'

'It's not that, Michael,' I said desperately. 'Irish imagination we need and fire and, and – inspiration, but even more, I think, the ferocity of the Turk and the sagacity of the Chinese. We need all of these qualities if we're really going to do graffiti on a plane, and you have them. I know you do.'

'So you want me to help you paint a plane?'

'We did talk about it in some detail last Sunday in the park.'

Now my stomach was really doing flip-flops, but Michael, when he spoke again, sounded much more normal, if that's the word for him. 'And so we did. Did you think I had forgotten? That's a good joke on you.'

It seemed to me that this depended on your sense of humor, but I hastily assured him that I had never thought any such thing.

'So you're ready, are you?' he went on. 'And you'll be standing by the hotline? Let me see. Every evening between six and seven. Can you all be near a phone for that hour every night?'

This sounded workable, since it was a time well after the end of school and also before any evening activities. 'We can and will,' I said. 'Call me first. Give me the time and place to meet, and I'll call the others.' Now my heart was joining my stomach in its mad gyrations. This was becoming all too real. I continued a little less bravely. 'Michael, are you sure you can do it? I mean, I should tell you that just a bit over an hour is as fast as we can do the piece, and that's a minor miracle. It really is.'

He was silent for an alarmingly long time. Then he said, 'Well, an hour it is then. If you tell me that's fast, Stevie, I'll have to believe it, but I'm glad you told me. I may have to give the matter some even more creative thought.'

'Would you like to see the piece and meet the other three artists?' I asked.

'No, lad, it's you I trust, right down to your furry toes. If you say your friends are fine artists and brave hearts, that's good enough for the old griffin. Just go on standby now, and you'll be hearing from me.'

'How long do you think – just at a very rough guess?' I asked before he could ring off.

'Lad, it might be tomorrow. It might be a month from tomorrow. It all depends on a lot of things.'

Good God. I didn't know which prospect was worse: instant action or an agonizingly endless wait. Somehow I managed to say a cheery and confident goodbye to my strange accomplice and hang up the phone before my nerves got out of control.

My mother came in with a bag of groceries as I was hopping madly from one foot to the other and tearing at my hair. 'Something the matter?' she asked.

'I'm having a psychomotor fit.'

'Oh well, if that's all,' she said mildly and started putting things in the fridge. Then she turned around and looked at me a little more closely. 'I haven't seen much of you lately,' she said, 'and what I see now is not reassuring. What have you been up to?'

'We've been painting a mural in Dorc's loft,' I said truthfully, 'and it's a hell of a big mural, and it's taken a lot more time than any of us thought it would. We're all exhausted.'

'Was there some kind of deadline?'

'It had to be finished last night, and we just made it,' I said. I could think of several elaborations on this theme, but not being a very accomplished liar, I always figure the less said the better.

Apparently my mother thought so too, because all she

said was, 'Well, I hope you'll get some more rest. You look like something has chewed you up and spat you out.'

'I've only got a week's worth of homework to do. But that won't take long,' I added brightly when I saw the expression on her face.

I went back to my room which, in spite of the waiting books, seemed like a refuge from a mad world. Maybe a spot of Sunday night television – something stimulating like 'The Wonderful World of Disney' – would help me concentrate. I fought off the feeling of despair which large quantities of dull homework always gave me and settled in to do it. As usual, it took less time than anyone would have thought possible. It also took the edge off my anxieties, so by ten o'clock I was again well and truly asleep.

CHAPTER 18

Anyone can imagine without any trouble at all what it was like to wait. I, for one, became more than usually hard to live with. Why go into the sordid details? The interval seemed like at least a geologic era but was, in fact, only eight days. On Monday, April 21st, at exactly six o'clock, just as I was giving my mother a graphic opinion of her plans for dinner, the phone rang. I snatched it off the hook and heard the voice of Michael O'Leary, alias Griffin Man, alias the Messenger of Doom.

'Steven, lad, are you ready?' it cried without preamble.

'Jesus, Michael. You've given me a heart attack,' I said. 'You mean this is it?'

'Verily and forsooth this is the night. Assemble the forces of darkness at the southeast corner of Sixty-fourth Street and Second Avenue, and we will wend our way across the Queensboro Bridge. The hour will be two of the morning, and the deed will be dire,' he finished with relish.

I looked out the window. The sun was going down in a cloudless sky.

'All right,' I said breathlessly, 'but Michael, are you sure? It's not a very dark and stormy night.'

'Lad, you can't have everything. The rest couldn't be better. Come on. Call your cohorts. I'll tell all when we meet.'

'We'll be there,' I said. 'Trust me, Michael.'

He chuckled. 'It's me you've got to trust now I think. Goodbye 'til later.'

I hung up the phone and turned to find my mother looking at me strangely. 'I've got to go out,' I said. 'I'm sorry about dinner. I'm sure it will be fantastic.'

'You're white as a sheet. Is something wrong?'

'Everything's fine. I just had a big surprise, and I have to go do something about it.' I was shifting from one foot to the other cursing the fact that the phone was in the kitchen. Enough of a dubious nature had already been overheard.

My mother confirmed this impression. 'Well, that certainly was a strange conversation,' she said, 'what I could hear of it.'

'Oh, he's just a weird guy,' I answered vaguely, and edging past her, I streaked for my room. There I pulled on an old navy blue sweatshirt and snatched up the hood to my black monk's robe. This had served me well on numerous Hallowe'ens. Tonight would be its finest hour. Jeans and purple sneakers were both dark enough, so I was as ready as I'd ever be.

We had left all our graffiti supplies at the loft, and I thought we could gather there and share out the load. There was plenty of time. I added my backpack, red but grimy, to the ensemble and shot out the door before any more questions could be asked. At some point I would call and say I was spending the night with Dorc.

I telephoned the others from the nearest booth, and each one answered with stunning promptness. Apparently I was not the only one who had been sitting on the phone for a solid hour every day for more than a week. I tried in these calls to be less hyper and more specific than Michael, but in view of my own excitement and nearly total lack of information, it wasn't easy.

Everyone made it to the loft by eight o'clock, which left us with about five hours to kill. This, in our state of nerves, was not a happy prospect. Sonia's suggestion that we do another run on the piece was greeted with the hostility it deserved. First we packed and repacked our various bags about ten times, like a bunch of maiden schoolteachers on their first trip to Europe. Then we played some pinball and drank a modest amount of beer.

'Better keep our reflexes fast,' Will said.

'And our bladders empty,' Dorc added.

'There must be plenty of pissing space on an airfield,' I said.

'You guys have all the luck there,' Sonia contributed.

And such was the level of wit with which we improved each shining hour. That sample is, I think, enough.

At ten Dorc consulted the TV Guide and found that there was a really appalling old horror flick on Channel Eleven. With 500 commercials it lasted until half-past twelve, and saved our sanity.

At this point there was nothing left to do but pick up our stuff and go. We wanted to allow plenty of time for the vagaries of the MTA, vagaries which increased markedly after midnight. Pausing for a moment at the door to the loft, I surveyed my friends.

'Well,' I said, 'you all look pale but determined – even Will.'

'Speak for yourself, white boy.'

'You have that sort of gray cast,' I added and was rewarded by seeing him pass his hand nervously over his face. Then he laughed and flung open the door.

'Onward and downward with the arts!' Will shouted, and we all ran wildly down the stairs and into the street, laughing and pushing, our spirits revived by action. We were on our way.

CHAPTER 19

While we were waiting for the Lexington at Broadway-Nassau, a transit cop came by, swinging his stick. There weren't any criminals in sight just then, and he was obviously bored to death and looking for someone to hassle. We pulled ourselves together into a semblance of respectability and tried to look pleased to find an arm of the law out so late for our protection. I felt as if X-ray eyes were boring into our knapsacks, brightening with vindictive glee at the sight of all those spray cans. I knew that in some parts of town a kid can't even take a paper-bag lunch into the subway without running the risk that some cop will stick his nose into it. My fears were groundless. The poor dude was merely bored, and perhaps we were a mildly interesting group.

Michael was late, and since none of us had ever seen his van, we jumped every time a remotely possible vehicle came down Second Avenue. There were a surprising number of them considering the time of night, or at least so it seemed by the time our particular one rolled up at two thirty. It was rcd, just as hc had said, dccrcpit, and depressingly small.

My friend came out of the driver's seat in one bound,

looking as wild and improbable as I had remembered. He stood by the door of the van, grinning hugely and swaying ever so slightly from side to side.

'Michael,' I cried. 'Good! You're here.'

'And where else would I be on this historic night? It's good to lay eyes on you again, my boy. These, I presume, are your fellow conspirators,' he added, as I shook his hand.

'Sonia, Will, Dorc, meet Michael, otherwise known as Griffin Man,' I said, and he shook hands with each of them.

'Now then,' he went on, 'we must see to the stowing of your persons and effects. For the greater part of our journey the young lassie and the hobbit may ride in front, since I have disposed of my partner for the night.'

'Your partner?' I said aghast. 'You never said you had a partner.'

'Well of course I have a partner,' Michael answered reasonably. 'You didn't think I did all this work myself – a born malingerer like me – did you now?'

'And what do you mean you disposed of him?' I said, my imagination taking its usual leap ahead of my intellect.

'Left him in the gents at Mulligan's Bar and Grill. What could be easier? That's why I'm a wee bit late. Thought the damn camel would never have to go, no matter how many rounds we had. Never mind that. The night is young.'

I looked around wildly at my friends, but they were laughing along merrily with this loon, and only I seemed to have any misgivings. Michael opened the back of the van and stowed our bags in the rear. When these had been followed by Dorc and Will, all the available space seemed to be full, but I supposed we could sit on top of them and that the last part of the ride would be short.

Sonia and I squeezed into the tiny cab with Michael. I was to have more physical contact with Sonia that night than in all the rest of our friendship put together. All that I lacked was the peace of mind to enjoy it. Fortunately, there was little traffic, which reduced the likelihood that I would be castrated every time Michael changed gears, and soon we were rolling smoothly along the expressway. It seemed at first that his driving was much less eccentric than one might have feared, but my relief was short-lived, for as soon as we were well under way, he pulled out a flask from some nook on his side of the van and began to tipple and to sing. The selection was a rousing traditional air which involved a lot of bravery and spilled blood. If this was intended to raise my spirits and prepare my heart for battle, it was not a success. Sonia and I perforce had our arms around each other, so we took what comfort we could in hugging through the performance, which lasted most of the way to the airport.

At last, with the lights of the field already winking in the darkness, we pulled off to the side of the road. Michael put his flask away and opened the door. 'Here's where you all really start playing sardines,' he said as Sonia opened her door and we both tumbled onto the pavement. Dorc and Will came out of the back stretching and groaning, and we formed a circle around our driver.

'All right, Michael,' I said sternly. 'This is the hour of truth. Where is it? What's it like? And, damn it, is that the full moon I see coming up over there?'

My three friends joined me in a horrified look at the large orange disk which was climbing above the low forms of the hangars, but Michael chuckled smugly. 'You're going to bless that moon, my children, because this plane is so far out I doubt you could see to paint without it. Now what you've got is a lovely 707. She's low enough to reach but quite big enough to suit your most grandiose designs. Besides this, we've been lucky in a more interesting way. You know that most east-bound planes leave at night because of the way the time change works – leave at night and arrive over there in the morning, which means they're serviced in the afternoon. Time is money more in the big plane business than in almost anything else; they've got to keep them in the air to make a buck.'

We all nodded a trifle impatiently at this lecture on airline economics, and Michael went on unperturbed: 'A few planes, however, do go to England in the early morning – England only, mind you. It's the closest place in Europe.' Now Michael grinned ferociously at the sight of our discontented faces. 'All right, you doubting Thomases!' he shouted in a terrifyingly loud voice. 'This plane is different. This plane, my friends, after dumping its routine lot of tiresome businessmen in London, is taking a small clutch of VIPs on to Cairo via Rome and Athens. Now what do you think of the old Griffin?'

'Hey, man,' Will breathed, and Sonia began to jump up and down.

'I think you are absolutely cosmic, Michael,' I said. 'But then, I always did.'

'So now all we have to do is go out there and get to it. Just like that,' Dorc said.

'That's all there is to it,' Michael answered cheerfully, 'but it may be that a wee scrap of contingency planning is in order.'

'Damn right it is,' Dorc said.

'If some little dinky thing drives up,' Michael continued, 'or if you hear me talking to one or even two men, don't panic. Remember, all that can be seen of you is your lower bodies. Just keep spraying and praying and trust to the old blarney. But if you hear sirens . . .' He paused dramatically and peered at us as if to be sure he had our attention. He did. 'If you hear sirens, brave hearts, run like hell for the van and jump in any way you can. I think I've got an escape hole located, and we will make for it without more ado. Now in you get and tally-ho.'

I don't know how we all got into the back of that tiny van with all the other stuff that was already there, and it would be useless to describe our contortions. You might as well try to tell someone what the Gordian knot looked like. Out of the pitch blackness after the door had closed came Dorc's voice, 'He *thinks* he knows an escape hole. Oh Jesus.'

'Come on, Dorc,' I mumbled into what seemed to be Sonia's midriff. 'The guy has accomplished miracles.'

'Quiet, everybody,' Will's voice commanded. 'When we reach that gate, there had better not be one tiny squeak in here or they'll open the door to check for mice.'

'No mice allowed on the airfield,' Sonia said, and she gave a slightly hysterical giggle.

The rest of us all said, 'Shhh!' at the same time, and silence fell, except for the roar and rattle of Michael's elderly van.

The passage through the guard post was much as I had imagined it in my horrible fantasy. Voices. Thumps. Presumably Michael was explaining the absence of his partner. The thumps remained unexplained and, of course, no one opened the rear door. It was still pretty frightening.

After that the ride got rougher, and it seemed to go on forever. I kept telling myself that the farther it was, the safer we would be, but I was still glad when we stopped. The door opened suddenly, ejecting the four of us onto the ground in a tangle. And there we sat for a moment staring up at the belly of what looked like the biggest goddamn plane in the world. Michael, however, was inside the van and had started throwing our precious bags at us.

'Michael!' I hissed, after catching one of them. 'Be careful, man.'

He came to the door and handed the last ones down, looking puzzled at our inactivity. The truth was that everything seemed so strange we were momentarily at a loss. The huge plane glimmered dully above our heads lighted only by the moon which was still low in the sky and by a few faint lights far away across the field. We were totally out of our element.

CHAPTER 20

Will was the first to recover. He jumped to his feet and started to pace along the side of the plane. The rest of us followed him. However short our time, we still needed to get the measure of the problem. Yes, the space was there and then some. We had a long strip under the windows and ahead of the wing which everybody but me could reach. Now Michael was handing down a sturdy box to make me even with the rest. Will started marking out the spaces, and the rest of us took up our bags, slipped into our places, and started to sketch. We were using medium gray markers which just barely showed, but they were enough to go by and would be covered by the final painting. Now that we were at work on our so-familiar task, the strangeness faded, though the tension remained. We were working fast and still getting used to the unfamiliar surface and the fact that it was a lot more of a reach than we were accustomed to. At the same time, nobody had forgotten that the uncanny peacefulness of the scene could hardly be expected to last.

Michael had been watching us, his teeth gleaming through his beard in a delighted smile. Now he produced his flask from somewhere and tipped back his head for a gigantic swig. 'And here's to ye, lass and laddies!' he roared. I almost fell off my box, and the others froze, petrified at this horrible sound, but nothing happened except that our mad friend went back to his van, chuckling, and drove around to the other side of the plane.

'Maria!' Sonia said. 'I wasn't even going to whisper.'

'An excellent rule, nevertheless,' Will said firmly, and we went back to work in silence.

From the other side of the plane we started to hear vague thumpings and scrapings as Michael began his appointed tasks. Occasionally, snatches of song also floated our way. We could only hope that this was his usual work style and would attract less attention than would more decorous behavior.

We had finished outlining the letters with dark spray paint and were ready to start fading and embellishing with color when we became aware of a light moving toward us on the other side of the plane. This was accompanied by the horrid sound of a small engine drawing rapidly closer.

'Don't stop,' Will said in a low, sharp voice. 'Work faster. Concentrate.'

Surprisingly, we all managed to obey. There was a loud scrambling noise as Michael dashed out of the plane and down the stairs to meet whatever challenge was upon him. The motor stopped, but the light stayed on and must have illuminated our lower parts in a blaze of glory. There were indistinguishable shouts. I don't think I have ever been so totally freaked out in all my life, but I drove my spray can onward. Might as well go down in action. Then a few words of Michael's came back sharp and clear: '. . . putting a new logo on. Silly bastards. What do they think . . .' The rest was lost. Sounds of conviviality followed. Michael must be sharing his flask. This was no doubt a splendid idea, but I thought it would never end. Finally a door slammed, a motor roared, and the light swung away from our legs and began to diminish as our visitor drove back toward the terminal.

I stopped for a moment because my hand was shaking. Next to me Dorc mumbled, 'Holy shit.' That seemed to sum it up for all of us.

By now the moonlight had become quite strong on our side, so we could really see what we were doing, and it was looking great. Our practice was paying off. Quite apart from the question of speed, I don't think we could have managed without it under these strange and bloodcurdling conditions. The only big problem continued to be the height we had to reach. I wished we had had the wit to practice a higher layout in the loft. It was going to take a lot of extra adrenalin to keep our arms from giving out, but then, extra adrenalin was not in short supply. After that last incident, sheer terror drove us on. It seemed unlikely that a second visitor could be so easily duped.

For a time, however, we were left in peace. Michael bumbled and bumped. We painted. We were just putting the last embellishments on when lights appeared again, and again the unwelcome growl of an engine began to grow across the field. We heard Michael curse and gallop down the stairs again. This time the voices were angry. It would seem a much less jolly dude had come upon the scene. Good God, they were coming around to our side. Michael was shouting, 'Just a stupid logo, you interfering son-of-a-bitch.'

'So I just want to see it, OK? I just want to see what the hell you're up to, O'Leary.' This was the other guy, and he sounded like someone I didn't want to meet.

A powerful flashlight suddenly came on blinding us so all we could see was that the man behind it was big. He was also alone except for our ally who was jumping up and down, waving his arms and shouting, 'Finish it! Finish it! He can't stop you.'

Will whirled around and took a step toward the intruder, and he was also big and suddenly very mean looking with his spray can held out like a weapon in front of him. I don't know what he would have done, but the man wasn't staying to find out. After all, we were five to one. He turned and dashed for his car.

'Drop everything and get in the van,' Michael shouted as the other vehicle tore off toward the terminal, but we hadn't tagged our piece yet, and there wasn't one of us who was willing to be anonymous at this point. We dropped our spray cans and grabbed our best wide markers. TOAD, ASTRA, DORC, SABRE 75. We signed ourselves with incredible care, so that no manic scribble marred those great and peaceful letters. Then we ran.

Sirens began to scream and lights to flash as Michael got his old heap under way. We roared off at suicidal speed, bouncing and rattling, the four of us shut up in the now nearly empty blackness of the van, clutching and falling on each other. Speech was impossible, and anyway we were speechless. Just as it seemed that all our bones would be broken, leaving nothing for our captors to do, the van came to a shattering halt and the doors were flung open. We were even farther out in the field than before. A chain link fence was about twenty yards ahead, and Michael took off for it like a rabbit, shouting for us to follow. He hit the fence and turned left, still running but a little more slowly. He was looking for a hole – the one he 'thought he had located'. Behind us the insane shriek of the sirens was growing by the second.

'This is it!' Michael yelled and dived for the ground. He was up in a flash on the other side of the fence, almost before we knew what had happened. Fortunately the hole was a good size, so no one got stuck. A Peter Rabbit crisis would have been the end.

Putting the fence between us and our pursuers had not stopped Michael. He was still running, this time to the right, toward a group of sheds. My short legs were beginning to make a difference, and none of my friends seemed concerned that I was being left farther and farther behind. Ahead of me, I saw them dive into the shadow of the first shed, while behind there was a great screeching of brakes as the police cars or whatever they were arrived at the abandoned van. Doors slammed. Lights flashed. I called up reserves I never knew I had and flung myself over the last few yards and into the shadow. For a moment I was lost. No one seemed to be there but me. Then I saw a shape sliding ahead of me in the nearly total darkness. It was Dorc, who seemed to be at the end of the line. He turned at the sound of my rasping breath and made a fierce, negative gesture. I gathered that I was to be quiet if I died in the attempt.

We slunk along some more, turned a corner, and stopped by the door to one of the buildings. Now I could vaguely discern all four of them standing close together. Michael opened the door but did not go inside.

'Can we hide in there?' Sonia whispered.

Michael shook his head. 'The door is a rather feeble red herring,' he said. 'We must hope that they will search all these buildings, which are poorly lighted and full of junk. Meanwhile, my friends, what we need most is a cab.'

'A cab,' Dorc said. 'Oh sweet Jesus, now he wants a cab.'

Michael, for once, did not stop to refute this slur on his sanity. Instead, he beckoned impatiently and began to slide away around another corner. We followed at a loss to think of anything better to do.

Quite soon we came out of the group of sheds on the opposite side from our point of entry. Now the buildings were between us and our pursuers, but their menacing shouts were still growing in volume. Before us ran one of the paved roads that carry the busy daytime traffic from one part of the airport to another. Upon its quiet face the moonlight lay and nothing else. Michael, however, advanced to the curb and stood there in the classic pose of one who awaits, with only modest urgency, a taxi cab. If I were asked to choose which of several moments during our ghastly adventure had been the worst, this would be a strong contender. There was nothing, absolutely nothing, we could do but stand and stare at Michael and the empty road while the sounds of pursuit among the sheds grew steadily closer.

Then suddenly we saw a pair of headlights, surmounted by a small yellow light, advancing upon us down the road. It was such an incongruous and homely sight that I had to stifle a hysterical giggle. We bounded up to Michael's side.

'There are always cabs cruising around this place,' he said in a conversational tone of voice. 'Day and night. It's remarkable.'

The cab drew up and the driver rolled down his window and surveyed us sourly. 'Can't take five,' he said. 'One of youse gotta stay behind.' Michael pulled out a ten dollar bill, which showed how out of touch he was with the real world of transportation. 'We wish to remain together,' he said flourishing his picayune offering.

The driver spat. 'Buddy, that's chicken shit this time of night.' He started to put his car in gear.

Will, however, with his usual sharpness in a financial crisis, had produced another ten. 'There's more where this came from,' he said, 'if you take all of us where we want to go.'

I looked over my shoulder and saw lights bobbing around, in and out of the sheds. Expressions of greed and suspicion were at war on the cabbie's unattractive visage.

'You guys in some kind of trouble?'

'Not at all,' Will said, and shoving both bills in the driver's face, he opened the back door, and we all piled in. It was another tight fit, but none of us wanted to start a discussion about riding in front. The answer probably would have been no anyway, since this cab had one of those partitions which are designed to protect the driver from the likes of us.

Fortunately, our surly savior decided to drive first and find out where second. As I glanced back through the rear window, three men with flashlights and, my God, drawn guns burst from between the sheds and ran to the side of the road. 'For Christ's sake,' I said softly. 'We could have been shot.'

'Quiet, hobbit,' Michael said and leaned forward to speak to the driver. 'Take us to Pan Am parking on the fourth floor.'

The cabbie, being a man of small imagination, did not seem to find this a strange request. 'I thought youse guys was goin' into the city,' he whined.

'For twenty bucks, you've got a bargain,' our friend answered severely.

'Michael, you maniac,' I hissed, hoping the driver couldn't hear me through the partition, 'why the hell aren't we going into the city? We could stop at my house and get some money if there isn't enough. This is no time to be chintzy.'

He twisted around and stared at me incredulously. 'I don't believe it,' he said. 'You of all people. Don't you want to see it fly?'

Dorc, who was at the bottom of the pile of bodies, gave a low moan, of physical or mental anguish, or both, but Sonia, predictably, was delighted. 'Oh fantastic, Michael,' she said. 'Can we really see it?'

'And why not, lass? We'll stand right up there and admire to our hearts' content.'

'But my God,' I cried. 'The airport. It's walking into the lion's mouth.'

'And where would the pigs be less likely to look?' asked Michael, who seemed to be indulging in even more rhetorical questions than usual.

'I say New York,' Dorc answered in a muffled shout. 'New York is where they're less likely to look, and New York is where I want to be.'

Michael did not even deign to reply to what he doubtless saw as a cowardly objection. There was a pause before Will finally said in a resigned voice, 'Let the madman have his way. He's gotten us this far unscathed.'

'If you don't count our ravaged minds,' I added, and we fell silent as the cab swung around to the Pan Am building and started up the ramp.

At the top, the cabbie left us and drove away as swiftly as the structure of the place permitted. It occurred to me that he was probably on his way to the nearest authority to report the presence of five dubious characters on the roof, and I said as much. Michael, however, was sure that the man would not want to discuss the fact that he had taken five people for an outrageous sum of money to such a curious destination. This sounded plausible if not totally convincing. I was suffering anyway from a kind of battle fatigue which numbed my awareness of danger. One can be just so scared for just so long, and then the nerves go on strike.

The parking lot was even spookier at this hour than it had been when I visited it on that far-away night of our reconnaissance. Gray light was seeping into the sky, and there was a pink line along the eastern horizon. We could begin to see each other's exhausted faces. It was cold, and Sonia and Dorc were huddled together. I wished I had a girl or a down parka or that I had never come. Already the painting on the side of the plane seemed distant and unreal. Michael passed his flask around. We waited and shivered as the daylight grew.

After about a century of this dismal inactivity, Michael looked at his watch, and walked briskly over to the side facing the field. 'Six o'clock,' he said. 'She should be trundling up any minute now.'

'I don't believe it's only been four hours since we were standing on that street corner,' Sonia said. 'My God, do you realize we hadn't even met this character four hours ago?'

'It's been a rich, intense relationship,' Dorc said.

'Here she comes!' Michael cried, and we gathered around him and peered off into the gloom. Our plane looked very small, way out there on the field, but now it was growing rapidly as it came towards us in the brightening light. It came in at an angle, and we could clearly see the immense, brightly colored letters that spelled 'peace' in four languages and three alphabets, before it turned its business side to the departure gate. Suddenly there were a lot of people running around our plane. Fists were shaken, heads were clutched, hair was torn, and we could even hear faint shouts from below. Words were not distinguishable, but we had no trouble imagining them. It was a splendid moment. No one felt cold any more, and no one even suggested trying to find a way to go home.

'This is a dicey moment,' Dorc said, after we had drunk our fill of the confusion below. 'Maybe they'll decide they can't fly anything so disgraceful.'

'I think that decision would have been made before she was brought up to the gate,' Michael answered, 'but we'll soon know the best or worst of it. Yes. Look. They're boarding all right. No time to bring in another plane, especially with those big cheeses wanting to get to their important business in Cairo. They probably don't care if their plane is pink with purple polka dots, so long as it flies.'

We laughed and hugged each other and hopped up and down until Will said, 'We'd better act a little more normal, if possible. Even up here, someone might wander by and wonder why so much excitement over the departure of one small airplane.'

'Small,' I said indignantly. 'It's humongous.'

Will, however, had tapped a hidden vein of common sense, and we managed to control our hilarity. Now, for our experience to be complete, we had to wait for the take off, and this would have been easier with a little horsing around. At the same time, to be caught at this point, because we were making asses of ourselves, would be absurd. We stood still. We waited. After this experience, I understood much better those accounts of great adventures which maintain that periods of waiting are much worse than the most hair-raising action.

At last the doors closed, and the roar of engines began. Slowly at first, and then with increasing speed, our plane turned out towards the runway. For a moment we were again able to glimpse our masterpiece before it fled away from us. I looked at the others' stricken faces. Sonia had tears in her eyes. 'It's gone,' she cried. 'I can't bear it.'

Michael held up his hand. 'Wait,' he commanded. 'Watch the sky.'

And now the roar of jets which had almost faded away was growing louder again. A sleek silver shape was sweeping towards us, airborne, catching the light of the rising sun. It banked before our eyes, and there was a stunning flash of color, the swift imprint of a bold design upon our minds. Then it was gone, out over the waves that tumbled for endless miles in the spring winds, off to London, Rome, Athens, Cairo. Speechless and motionless we watched it go, and the thought passed through my mind that I would be lucky if even once again in my life I could feel this grand.

The curiously matter-of-fact voice of Griffin Man broke the spell. 'And now,' it said, 'I will call another cab.'

I hope it is enough to say that this ridiculous method of getting away from Kennedy airport worked. The cab was large, the driver sleepy and incurious. We passed unrecognized from the scene of our triumph, each of us, I am sure, with the same thought in his numbed brain, that a lifetime supply of luck had been used up in one night. If so, it seemed at the time to be well worth the sacrifice. I, for one, hoped never to need so many gods on my side again.

EPILOGUE

CROWDS ROAR AS GRAFFITI JET ROLLS IN
Ta Nea (Athens)

NOT RESPONSIBLE.
PAN AM DISOWNS PAINTED PLANE
New York Daily News

BRAVA NEW YORK! UN MESSAGGIO
DI PACE GRAFFITO SU UN JET
Corriere della Sera

MYSTERY MESSAGE ON PLANE
DISMAYS TRAVELLING DIPLOMATS
Guardian

GRAFFITI JETS ABROAD
Village Voice

CAIRO SHOCKED AT GAUDY US PLANE
Al-Ahram

MESSAGE OF PEACE FROM NY YOUTH
STUNS THE WORLD
International Herald Tribune

GRAFFITI PLANE MEETS MIXED REACTION
The Times (London)

NY KIDS TRASH PLANE
Athens Daily Post

GRAFFITI ON PLANE SEEN AS
MESSAGE FROM NEW YORK YOUTH
Some Evidence of Social Conscience, Experts Contend
The New York Times

LO STILE SUBWAY
SU UN VOLO INTERNAZIONALE
Il Messaggero

KIDS DEFACE JET
FURIOUS KOCH VOWS REVENGE
New York Post

We would probably never have known about the foreign headlines if we had not, in fact, been caught. It happened in a ridiculous and diverting way – not, as you might think, because Dorc had written his real name on the other side of the plane, but through my own reckless habit of putting my tag all over my portfolio.

I was standing just inside the school entrance one day, about a week after the great event, looking for a friend and trying, as usual, to keep from being trampled to death, when a deep, soft voice said, 'Well, well, so *this* is Sabre 75. Whoever would have believed it?'

There was no mistaking the knowledge behind that voice, and when I looked up and saw the man who had spoken, I immediately abandoned the various stories which had flashed through my mind. He was simply not going to believe that I was carrying someone else's portfolio, or that I had copied a more famous kid's tag, or anything but the grisly truth. He was one of those perfectly turned out young black guys who start at the bottom in places like *The New York Times* and don't stop scrambling up the ladder until they drop. The fact that it had taken him a week to find me was nothing – the merest drop in the well of his determination. I was putty in his hands, and so were my accomplices once he had conned me into producing them.

In the end it all turned out remarkably well. The reporter who found me had been an inmate of our school himself for a while. He not only knew where to look for graffiti artists, he also had some feeling for what made us tick. The publicity that followed was embarrassing but certainly not without its agreeable moments.

After the amused enthusiasm displayed by much of the foreign press and the submerged but still evident admiration of *The New York Times*, the question of punishment did not arise. New screams of outrage were heard, of course, and also some fairly thunderous rounds of applause. My parents and Giorgio Feltrinelli laughed themselves sick. Sylvia, and Sonia's parents, looked bewildered. And in the naturally censorious eye of the judge there appeared, if Will is to be believed, a brief but unmistakable gleam of mischievous delight.

Sonia's brother Carlos reacted somewhat differently. He tracked us to the loft and came in one night unannounced, when we were all there lying around on beanbags and admiring our piece, which still adorned the wall. I suppose Sylvia must simply have stood aside in open-mouthed wonder at the sight of so much ethnic magnificence on her doorstep. Anyway, suddenly, there he was in our midst. He stalked over to the wall and gazed in long and menacing silence at our work. Then he whirled upon us with a dazzling smile. 'Amigos!' he cried. 'You are now members of Carlos's gang. We will do great things together, you and I.'

Flattered but reticent might describe our reaction to this honor. At that time a good rest on our laurels seemed the most attractive prospect.

Michael O'Leary was for the moment subsisting happily on unemployment benefits. These splendid funds seem to be available no matter what you do to lose your job. I still felt guilty about him, however, and had given him my bestiary as a small gesture of gratitude. This, he said, as he sat swigging and sketching by the Statue of Alice, was more than enough for him – this and the memory of a glorious deed.

Some other titles in Puffin Plus

THE WRITING ON THE WALL

Lynne Reid Banks

A totally convincing and unpatronising novel about the contemporary dilemmas facing an intelligent but innocent young girl.

EASY CONNECTIONS

Liz Berry

Cathy's vision of the future is shattered when she meets Paul Devlin, the lead guitarist with the rock group Easy Connection and a millionaire superstar. A powerful love story.

IS ANYONE THERE?

ed. Monica Dickens and Rosemary Sutcliff

A collection of stories and articles about some of the difficulties and uncertainties encountered by young people. Originally published to celebrate 25 years of the Samaritans.

THE VILLAGE BY THE SEA

Anita Desai

A moving story about two teenagers facing an out-of-work father, a seriously ill mother and two little sisters too young to help or understand.

SUMMER OF MY GERMAN SOLDIER

Bette Greene

In wartime Arkansas, a Jewish girl befriends a German prisoner on the run. A most unusual and moving story.

BIKER

Jon Hardy

There's more to being a despatch rider than meets the eye! The atmosphere, speed and toughness of life riding the streets of London is captured in this fast-moving and eventful series of five episodes.